HEARTS ON
HEALING SOULS

Dixie Lynn Dwyer

MENAGE EVERLASTING

Siren Publishing, Inc.
www.SirenPublishing.com

A SIREN PUBLISHING BOOK
IMPRINT: Ménage Everlasting

HEARTS ON FIRE 6: HEALING SOPHIA
Copyright © 2016 by Dixie Lynn Dwyer

ISBN: 978-1-68295-210-8

First Printing: May 2016

Cover design by Les Byerley
All art and logo copyright © 2016 by Siren Publishing, Inc.

Printed in the U.S.A.

PUBLISHER
Siren Publishing, Inc.
www.SirenPublishing.com

DEDICATION

Dear readers,

Thank you for purchasing this legal copy of Hearts on Fire Healing Sophia.

The decisions we make in life sometimes aren't the smartest. Perhaps we make decisions based on the mood we're in, the words exchanged that convince us to choose one thing over another. Or the power of persuasion.

Sophia is no different. Young, easily manipulated by an older, hero figure type man, she chooses a path that leads to heartache, abuse and ultimately—the potential for death.

Because of that negativity and fear, she cannot trust, cannot believe in someone's word or promises of safety and security. She has a hardened heart and it will take some very special men to help her trust again.

May you enjoy Sophia's journey as she overcomes her fears, finds a creative, successful way of removing visible scars and turn them into beauty, and ultimately find healing in the arms of her four Navy SEALs.

Happy reading.

Hugs!

~Dixie~

HEARTS ON FIRE 6: HEALING SOPHIA

DIXIE LYNN DWYER
Copyright © 2016

Prologue

Eight Months Earlier

"You want to leave me? You want to toss away all our plans and the money, the status?" Mateo yelled at Sophia.

"What status? From who, Mateo? Your gang-banging buddies? Your fellow business friends, corrupt cops, politicians, attorney friends who work the system and screw over the laws they are supposed to uphold? What status do you mean?" she yelled at him.

The backhand came out of nowhere. It was so sudden and precise it sent her into the table. She grabbed onto the edge, stopping herself from falling.

She tasted the blood by her lip, and anger boiled in her belly.

She looked at his friends. They weren't any better than him. The power, the money, all went to their heads, too. The other people pretended not to notice him striking her. She was tired of this shit. Tired of being treated like a piece of property and tired of the way other men looked at her, touched her shoulder, or hugged her and sniffed her hair. Mateo did nothing to stop them. In fact, it was almost as though it turned him on, seeing other men want her. Deavan, his right-hand man, his partner, was no different. When he looked at her she felt nothing but trepidation and intense concern. God help her. She needed out of this relationship. She needed her life back.

Now he'd caused a scene. His little celebratory party had turned into a show for his peeps, as he liked to jokingly call them. He was supposed to be a good guy, a higher-up in the correctional facility, a man who kept bad guys behind bars, but instead, he used his badge, his prison connections, and his old neighborhood connections to gain money and power on the streets. She had been so stupid to believe he was making good money working at the correctional facility doing overtime and assisting the warden. He was working the system, and so were his friends. They had connections to drugs, prostitutes, and money. He was more than a bookie and a loan shark. He was capable of so much more, and she had seen him push the limit. He was a lunatic, and he believed that he could get away with anything. She'd had enough.

She watched two of the women next to one of his friends stare at Mateo. Mateo looked at them with hunger in his eyes, and she knew he was cheating on her. Why was she here still? What was it he wanted from her? She should call him out on his indiscretions. She should tell him to go to hell and take the whores with him, but how could she? She was nothing now and had nothing but her small bank account and her little secretary job working part time for someone he knew and trusted. He didn't even want her working at the larger real estate offices downtown. He'd made her quit her job, and she'd fallen for his possessive, controlling behavior coated with kisses, finger fucks, and the techniques he used to play her body like a professional. But even that had started to feel wrong. She couldn't stay with a man who didn't love her, who didn't put her first and who could smack her in front of a crowd of friends and whores.

Her temper flared.

"I'm finished." The tears rolled down her cheeks, and she used the back of her hand to wipe the blood from her lip. She was shaking. She knew the consequences of talking back. She didn't care so much, not with those women checking out the man who was supposed to be hers and hers only. Funny thing was she didn't want anything to do with him. She didn't want to be in his bed, under him, or on top of him. She wanted to be loved and cherished. He wanted a servant, a member of his new team and group of criminal minds, and a pretty face and sexy body by his side that other men drooled over and wanted.

She needed to be more than that.

She slowly walked toward the door, and then Deavan stood in front of it. He was one of Mateo's right-hand men. A big guy who stood over six feet tall and weighted over two hundred pounds. He was a combination of fat and muscle, a bouncer type, but was quick and capable.

She saw his expression. She wouldn't be allowed to leave unless Mateo gave the okay. She wouldn't make complete eye contact with Devan. He might think it was an invitation to touch her more and take a taste of her. At this rate, the way Mateo had been acting, he could let Deavan or even Jeremy have her, too. She felt sick.

She glanced back at Mateo. A quick look told her he had dismissed the other people from the room, and she was left with Mateo, Deavan, and Jeremy.

Mateo lit the candle on his desk. He stared at the flame.

"Let me go, Mateo. I want to leave."

He ignored her request, and she swallowed hard. Mateo pulled out a black case. She gasped.

No. Oh God no.

Mateo smirked at her. Her expression acknowledged what was in that case and what it meant. She knew what he intended to do, but why her? Why would he want to make her his possession when he'd obviously cheated on her?

He's going to brand me. Force me to be his woman forever. He's staking a claim.

"Come to me, Sophia."

She shook her head.

"It's not a request. I think you need a reminder about who you belong to." Mateo pulled out the small metal branding stick. It was a six-inch, flat metal iron prod, a circle with the letter M in the center. The sick bastard had branded his closest friends, his peeps, as he liked to call them. It was part of an initiation and bond. Mateo owned them, and he'd wanted to own her since day one over a year ago. She had been so stupid.

She gasped as the hands landed on her waist from behind.

Deavan pressed close to her.

"Go to him, Sophia. He's been more than patient." He squeezed her hips as if he had every right to do so and to touch her like that. When he pushed her closer to the table where Mateo was, she tried planting her feet and Deavan's arm came around her waist, his hand right below her breast.

"Hold her tight," Mateo stated firmly. His dark brown eyes remained transfixed to the branding tool as he held it over the flame.

"No, Mateo, please don't do this. I don't want this."

"You have no choice. You belong to me. To us," he said, and her eyes widened as she glanced toward Jeremy, who moved closer.

"What?"

Jeremy just stared at her. She thought he looked upset, maybe like he didn't agree with this, as his eyes widened and he took several uneasy breaths. It was just a feeling, but she didn't think he condoned this one bit.

"Why are you doing this? It's obvious you've cheated on me, God knows how many times. Brand one of your whores who will bow down at your command. I don't want this, and I don't want you."

The forearm came down hard to the back of her neck. She cried out as Deavan slammed her against the desk.

She struggled to get free. His teeth nipped her neck, making her shudder and freeze.

"Ours. We're brothers, branded as one," Deavan told her, whispering into her ear.

She panicked and kicked her legs. They hit the table, and she pushed with all her might against the wood. Deavan stepped back, losing his balance momentarily, and then he slammed her forward. Her chest and face hit the table. Deavan pressed over her from behind. Mateo gripped her hands and held them down against the wood.

"No. Stop please. Please don't do this to me," she cried out, but they didn't listen. Instead, hands lifted her dress and unzipped the back, exposing her bare back.

Deavan squeezed her ass cheeks.

"Fuck, Mateo, you lucky bastard. She's got a great ass. Should we brand her there?" he asked as he manipulated his fingers along her curves.

Mateo held her wrists with one large, strong hand and caressed down her back to her ass then back up again.

"How about here, on her shoulder, so when she wears one of those strapless dresses everyone will know she belongs to you?"

"Or right here, above her ass, on her lower back? What a sight to see while we're fucking her," Deavan suggested.

She was crying and shaking with terror. Why was this happening to her?

Mateo stood up. "I like your thinking, Deavan. Hold her down."

He gripped her hair and turned her head upward in an awkward position.

"Ouch. Oh God, Mateo, please don't hurt me. Please. I won't leave. I'll stay, I promise."

He leaned down close to her lips. "You will stay. You belong to me, to us. We're your family now, Sophia. No others exist but us. When I do this, it means you're mine forever."

He plunged his tongue into her mouth kissing her brutally hard.

As he released her lips, he pulled back, pressed his palm over her back as Deavan gripped her tighter.

Then came the excruciating pain.

She cried out until she had no voice, and then suddenly she passed out.

* * * *

"This is a fucking serious situation. Scaggs wants a piece of the action," Jeremy whispered to Mateo as he caressed Sophia's hip and ass in bed. The place where Mateo branded her was enflamed, raw looking, and painful. Jeremy knew first-hand how it felt, and he was three times her size. He wished there had been something he could have done about it, but blowing his cover wasn't an option. Not now. Not after two full years working undercover, one year prior getting the connections to finally hook up with Mateo, and gaining this asshole's trust. Mateo Ruiz was going down.

"He'll have to wait in line like the others," Deavan contributed to the conversation as he stood by the doorway watching. He wanted Sophia, too. It was sick.

When Mateo had found her, working in a club part time while trying to earn her real estate license, trying to make ends meet on her own, he'd wined and dined her, winning over her heart like some prince in shining armor. She was virginal, twenty-two, all alone, and Mateo took advantage of all of it. He told her he was a correctional officer, a man who helped ensure that bad men who committed crimes were kept behind bars. He made it seem glamorous, impressive, and noble. Mateo was already working the system and gaining the trust of some big-time assholes. Coming across Mateo's involvement in illegal criminal activity had been like hitting a gold mine for the federal agents.

But just as they planned on taking him and his crew of shit out of the equation and ending their little business, they caught wind of some even bigger fish finding interest in Mateo's operations. The heads of the task force put on the brakes for the raid. Three weeks later, and after some very in-depth training and background studying, Jeremy went in undercover. Two fucking years and now three major drug dealers were part of the business, a shitload of government employees who worked for the correctional facilities in the state of Illinois and about a dozen others. If everything worked out accordingly, the feds would have them all indicted, arrested, and locked up among the scum they'd aided these last two years.

"I'm not too worried about Scaggs," Mateo said. "He knows that he needs me to keep negotiations open and to deal with the buyers. They don't trust him or any of the other more publically known bosses Besides, from what I've heard through some of my sources, Scaggs is on the feds' radar. We don't need to take any chances." Mateo ran his hand along Sophia's ass. He leaned down and kissed her skin then kissed along her back, avoiding the damage he'd made, and then to her shoulders. He trailed a hand along her breast, cupping it and playing with her body right there in front of them while the poor woman slept. He'd given her something during the night when she awoke from passing out and was in pain. Jeremy didn't know what it was, or what Deavan and Mateo had done to her during the night, but she was still out cold, and there were marks on her arms and her legs.

Mateo's words got him to refocus on the investigation and what needed to be done sooner than later in order to save Sophia and put Mateo in jail.

"Where did you hear about the feds looking at Scaggs? He keeps all his deals on the down low."

"That's what we all thought, but then Deavan here has been doing a little undercover work himself. Seems someone tipped off the feds on a few deals."

Jeremy glanced at Deavan, who held a firm, non-emotional expression. Jeremy didn't like how his gut clenched.

"And you've known about this how long and didn't tell me?" Jeremy asked and gave Mateo the meanest look. Meanwhile he couldn't help but to think they were on to him. He needed to keep his cool. He had been very careful. He knew he had to be.

Mateo looked at him and then at Deavan as Deavan sat down on the bed and caressed Sophia's long brown hair.

"It's not your worry. This is Deavan's job right now."

"So what would you like me to tell Scaggs? No deal?"

"I'll take care of it," he said, and then Sophia began to awaken.

She moaned and blinked her eyes open.

Deavan caressed her cheek.

"Hey, beautiful," he whispered, and Mateo didn't bat an eye.

Sophia tightened up, cringed from the pain, and turned slightly, trying to cover her breasts. Her gaze darted from Deavan to Jeremy then to Mateo. That was when Jeremy saw the bruising along her thighs. She crunched up into the fetal position, and Jeremy feared that Mateo and Deavan had raped her last night. He had disappeared to meet up with Scaggs and negotiate a possible deal. Then he'd made contact with his fellow agents and they planned a raid around this deal between Mateo and Scaggs. But his gut was warning him that Mateo and Deavan were on to him and knew he was working undercover.

"You should have stuck around last night, Jeremy. Sophia is really special, and very sweet." Deavan leaned down and licked along her shoulder. She shuddered and clenched her eyes closed.

"Someone had to meet with Scaggs. Besides, I like my women conscious when I fuck them," Jeremy stated firmly, getting an angry look by Deavan.

"She belongs to the three of us now, but she needs to learn her place. She needs rules," Mateo said and gave her ass a smack before he climbed out of the bed and stepped into his jeans.

"Breaking her in will be a lot of fun," Deavan said and glided his hand along her ass and thighs then between her legs from behind.

"No." She moaned in a very hoarse voice as she tried moving away from him.

Deavan gripped her thigh, and she gasped in pain.

"I thought we went over things last night, Sophia," Mateo said. "You need to adjust to the fact that you belong to me, Deavan, and Jeremy now. This body is ours to do with as we please when we please. Now rest so you're more than ready for the three of us tonight." Mateo looked at Jeremy.

Jeremy felt sick, angry, and wanted to kill both men right now. But he couldn't. He had to be patient, and it sounded as if Deavan hadn't forced sex on her last night because of her injuries and the drugs Mateo had given her. But he had obviously touched her, and that really disgusted Jeremy. He didn't think he could stand by and see the young woman get abused any longer. Something had to give. Setting up this deal with Scaggs and Mateo could break the case wide open and end this whole operation.

"I'll call Scaggs and set something up to meet," Mateo told him.

"You're going to deal with him? Give him a percentage of operations?" Jeremy asked, and Mateo stared at him.

"I'll let you know. But you'll be busy taking care of something else that's very important to us."

"What's that?" Jeremy asked.

Mateo glanced at Sophia, who was crying, as Deavan continued to touch her against her will. He was a big man too, way over six feet tall, and he was huge. On top of Sophia, he covered her body entirely.

Jeremy swallowed hard and bit the inside of his cheek. He couldn't let his emotions and disgust show. It would get him and Sophia killed.

"Our special young lady. Sophia. Watch over her. She's in a fragile state, and I can't focus on her right now when I've got all these deals going on and Scaggs to meet."

Jeremy thought about that a moment and then decided this was a better way to stay clear and take Mateo down. He wouldn't be near the location when the feds raided the meeting. He could get Sophia out of here so she was safe, and his cover wouldn't get blown too soon.

"Fine, but just know, for the record, that I would rather be at the meeting making sure things go smoothly. After all, I have been doing this for quite some time, and babysitting a woman isn't my forte."

Mateo reached out and clutched Jeremy's shoulder, giving him a smug-looking grin.

"Just think, if she acts up, you can begin fucking her into submission. I won't mind at all. You and Deavan are my brothers now." He ran his hand along Jeremy's forearm where the M branded in his skin was.

Jeremy clenched his teeth but held Mateo's gaze. He'd never wanted to kill someone so badly in his life.

"Plus Deavan has been getting her body used to his touch since last night. So when he takes her, she'll be more than ready. You do the same." He winked, and Jeremy nodded, but inside, he wanted to rip Mateo's heart out and feed it to him.

Justice would prevail. Sophia would be saved.

* * * *

Sophia was in a panic as she got out of the shower and got dressed. Jeremy was here watching her, and Mateo and Deavan would be back any time. The son of a bitch had branded her with his mark, and it was so painful. It burned, and she was stuck with it forever. She felt so violated and disgusted. Plus, when she'd awoken and felt and saw Deavan touching her, she wanted to vomit. Had they raped her? She didn't even know. They'd drugged her, and her thighs and groin had bruises on them, and she couldn't remember how they got there. Then, while in pain and still under the influence of drugs, Deavan had touched her intimately, and there had been nothing she could do about it. She wanted to die. She was so scared, and now Jeremy was here. He was watching her and kept looking at his cell phone and asking if she felt okay and stronger. She was confused.

The bathroom door swung open, and she screamed.

"We need to go. Now," he yelled at her, and she didn't want to go but felt so defeated. She was stuck here with three men who would rape her, abuse her, and kill her if she disobeyed them. She started to cry, and Jeremy cupped her cheek.

"I know you're scared, honey. I need you to listen to me and find it in your gut to trust me right now. Please, Sophia. You need to trust me, and I promise I'll save you and this will all be behind you."

She didn't know what to say or to do. Her instincts were shit, that was obvious, but there was something different in Jeremy's eyes. As soon as he saw her expression change with her thought, he gave her a nod.

"You're so fucking strong. You'll get through this and have a real life. Have a man who will love you. You'll see. Now follow me."

He took her hand and pulled her along. They exited the door in the large apartment He looked around and then brought her down the hallway to an elevator. It wasn't a main one. It was a service elevator.

"What are we doing?"

He didn't answer, and she was shaking so hard she wondered if he was taking her somewhere so he could have her himself. She trusted no one. She was in a panic. Her hands were shaking as she hugged herself and tried to figure out what to do. She couldn't get away. Even if she escaped from Jeremy, she couldn't trust the police. Mateo owned people in that profession and others. She was screwed.

They entered the elevator, and he looked at his phone.

"Fuck, fuck, fuck," he exclaimed.

The doors opened, and they were in the parking garage.

He grabbed her shoulders. Sirens blared in the distance.

"Jeremy?"

He shook his head

A card skidded near them, a black SUV with black-tinted windows.

"Trust me," he said to her.

The door opened, someone pulled her inside, and they took off in the SUV, her inside with five men.

"Miss Brown, we're special agents with the federal government. You're safe now. We'll explain everything once you're at a secure location," one of the men told her, and she couldn't believe what was happening. She wondered whether it was real or not. What had Jeremy done? Why? What about Mateo and Deavan?

She didn't know until four hours later when Jeremy arrived at the hotel looking like a dead man walking.

Chapter 1

Present Day

"Holy shit! It is so great to have you back," Hal "Hollywood" McCurran said to his friend Cerdic.

"It's great to be back. Six years was way too long," Cerdic replied then took a slug of beer from his bottle of Bud.

"Your brother Andreas seems a little happier. I think I caught a smirk before from him," Nate Hawkins added to the conversation, and then he took another slug of beer.

"Yeah, well, it's nice to be back to civilian life and not dodging bullets in the field," Cerdic replied.

"Treasure Town may not have people taking potshots at first responders in uniform, but you and Gideon will get your fair share of action on the water doing marine patrol," Hal told him, and then Gideon walked over.

"Damn, the Station has not changed one bit," Gideon said to them.

"Yeah, well, Dad and Jerome have a way of running the business," Billy McCurran added.

"Yeah, they sure do have some good-looking bartenders. Especially that sweet-looking brunette right there," Gideon told Bear.

"Watch it, Gideon, that's our woman," Hal said very seriously, and Gideon and Cerdic chuckled.

"We heard. Congratulations, guys. I can't believe that Jake finally settled down. Where is your local sheriff?" Gideon asked.

"He's around. Probably still shooting the shit with Lew."

"How is Lew holding up after that gunshot wound? We had no idea he was even injured," Hal said.

"He didn't want anyone to know. That's Lew. As commander for years, he runs things and always wants to be in charge. Thought he was damn invincible until that sniper got him in the chest," Gideon stated.

"But since he can't work active duty for the police department or marine patrol like me, Andreas, and Gideon can, he's planning on running the maintenance on those two townhouses and the beach house we invested in. He'll be the landlord, the service guy that gets called for any problems by the tenants," Cerdic told them.

"Tenants better not complain much, or he'll kick them out. That man still short in the patience department or what?" Bear asked.

"Still short, but if you guys know anyone looking, send them our way. Both places are still available for rent right now," Cerdic told them.

"Will do," Hal said, and they continued talking.

Cerdic looked around the place and truly felt at home in Treasure Town. Nights were still bad for the four members of his team. All Navy SEALs, all members of this community where they'd grown up as kids and best friends for life. They'd been inseparable from the start, and being in combat together, working secret missions, and sharing everything was perfect. He watched his old friends greet their women, who joined them. Each of them seemed to have landed pretty good-looking women, and they all seemed happy. It made him think that having such a committed relationship could work for him and the team, too. But not now. Not with them all having to adjust to working regular jobs, reestablishing their capabilities as marine patrol personnel, and following the rules of the land and not the rules of soldiers trying to survive with enemies everywhere.

Yep, they were back in town, back home where they belonged and in one piece somehow. He looked for Lew and spotted him still talking to Jake McCurran, along with a few other friends. His expression was hard, and he barely smiled. It would take some time. He'd been a prisoner behind enemy lines for over a week's time before they'd found him and rescued him. Getting shot and nearly dying had taken its toll on Lew. He needed to feel safe, secure, and like his team had his back instead of him being the one to always have theirs. Cerdic was just fine with that. He could have lost him, and that just wasn't an option any of them could have lived with.

"To Treasure Town and to the marine patrol," Andreas said as he raised his beer bottle.

They all raised theirs, too, and cheered before taking slugs from their bottles and resuming their talk about the old days. Everything was going to be just fine. Cerdic was certain they'd made the right decision in coming here. No regrets, just opportunity for further happiness.

* * * *

Nate Hawkins and his brother Rye were working on putting a new deck on someone's beach home near the channel. They had a couple of more days of work left, and they wanted to finish things up. They were ending their day and packing up the truck with supplies and tools when his cell phone rang.

"Is it Frankie?" Rye asked, knowing that she had gone to the beach with some friends today. Neither Nate or Rye, or their brothers Turbo and Mike, liked her out of their sight. It wasn't that they didn't trust her. It was how protective they were over her as their woman, especially after all they had gone through recently.

"No, I don't recognize the number." Nate answered it anyway.

"Nate, Jay Black."

"Jay? Holy shit, how are you buddy?" Nate asked, shocked to hear from his old friend from the agency. They'd worked in one of the special units for years, and then Jay had been transferred. They'd lost touch.

"In a bit of a jam. I need a favor, bud. I know you're retired and all, but it's personal. I need a safe house for a while."

"Shit. For you?"

"No. A woman."

"Fuck."

"Tell me about it. It's serious. I've transferred her to several places. Can't get into the details, but a raid backfired. The arrests fell through, and my cover has been blown. A two-fucking-year operation shot to shit, and I can't resolve this while keeping her under my wing." Jay finally exhaled.

"Sounds pretty serious. Will she need full security, armed and on lookout?" Nate asked, and Rye widened his eyes.

"This guy who is after her could be anywhere. He and his buddy dropped off the face of the planet. My hope is that he's long gone, out of the country, but I doubt it. I'll give you more info in a day or so. What you need to know is that this woman has been through hell. She's only twenty-three, and I need to know that she'll be safe until the agency can re-gather their evidence, collect some more, and locate these assholes who want her. The agency had a rat in it, and until I can figure out who that is, she and I are as good as dead."

"What are you going to do? Where will you stay?"

"I think it's best we separate. This asshole and his buddies believe Sophie is theirs. The main guy was obsessed with her, and he did things, Nate."

Jeremy got quiet, and Nate knew it was bad. He didn't want to think about all the possibilities from his own experiences with criminals and working cases for the government. He thought about his woman and swallowed hard.

"It's a long story. I can explain more later on. Do you think you have a location and some people who can keep an eye on her for me until I figure this shit out? I know that town you live in is super special. She needs good people around her. People she can trust or, at least, learn to."

"Sure thing. You know I'll do my best to watch over her and keep her safe. When should I expect the package to arrive?"

"Thanks, buddy. By noon time tomorrow. I'll contact you with more info. I owe you big time."

Jeremy disconnected the call, and Nate looked out toward the development and the beach. He was already forming a plan in his head and coming up with possible locations.

"What's going on? Who is in trouble, and what do we need to do?" Rye asked, and Nate felt the love for his brother fill his heart.

"That was a buddy of mine from the agency."

Rye crossed his arms in front of his chest and gave him a serious expression.

"And?"

"And he needs help in providing a safe location for a young woman in trouble. I don't know all the details, but it sounds pretty bad. Especially since my buddy says the men that are after her are after him. A raid went wrong, and his cover got blown. We need to provide a safe location for this woman."

"Shit. Did he indicate how protected she has to be? I mean we have Francesca and our brothers to think about too, never mind friends and the community here."

"I know that. Believe me I do. Jeremy wouldn't ask me to provide a safe house for this woman if he thought the men looking for her would figure it out and come here. It sounds temporary. I'll get more information from him later. Right now I need to figure out where I can place her and who could watch over her. I wouldn't want to just put her in a rental or something with no one around. I need to think about this a bit and maybe call Jake."

"Jake would have a good idea where to bring this woman. Besides, as sheriff, he should be aware of this situation."

"Yeah, but no one else, Rye."

"I understand. I'm here if you need some help."

Nate nodded, and they continued to put the rest of their supplies into the truck.

His mind was heavy on thinking of a place they could put this woman, and then his cell phone rang again.

He looked at Rye, who seemed on edge. He couldn't blame him. His brother knew how serious Nate's job had been for the government. He didn't ask questions.

"Hello?"

"Hey, Nate, it's Lew. I've got a freaking ceiling fan in the bathroom of this rental by our house that isn't working. I can't rent this place if there's mold on the walls caused by the fan not working. But I went into the attic, and I can't figure this shit out. Any way you could help me?"

Nate thought about it a moment, along with the facts that Lew and his brothers were retired Navy SEALs and their rental place was right next door to their own personal house. They also had the two townhouses they were renting, but they were blocks away.

"Not a problem. And besides fixing that fan, I may have a renter for you, if it's still available."

"That's great. Who is it?"

"I'll explain when I get there. Your team going to be around too?" Nate asked.

"Oh shit. Yeah, they will be. I'll make sure," Lew said, totally understanding Nate's tone.

Nate had known these men for years, they were good at their jobs, and they were trustworthy. The only thing was that they were hardcore, and they might not be interested in being part of this situation considering they were retired and Lew had been shot and nearly killed. But what choice did Nate have? He needed people he trusted and a safe location. Things could just fall into place.

"Lew, the fewer people that know, the better it is. I'll want to come by and look over the place, the surrounding homes and landscape to ensure safety."

"A safe house, huh? I get what you're saying. We're right next door, Nate. Even with the guys' schedules with the marine patrol, I'll mainly be around."

"Not sure if babysitting is necessary, just security and peace of mind. That could change, Lew. Like I said, I don't have much info. Yet. I hate throwing this into your lap."

"No you don't. You know as well as I do that transitioning into civilian life sucks, and this is what my team and I are good at. We'll do our best."

"I know you will. Rye and I will be there in about twenty minutes to fix that fan situation at the house. Then we'll all head to the house you're renting in the cul-de-sac by your place."

"I'll wait for you guys here. Thanks."

Chapter 2

Sophia looked into the mirror, turning sideways to see how the branding looked. Surprisingly it wasn't as raised and sore looking as it had been the weeks before. With each week that passed, it healed, but it was there forever, as a constant reminder of Mateo and his hurtful, sick control. Jeremy had suggested she get a tattoo to cover it, and that there were really great tattoo artists that could disguise the branding so no one would even notice. As soon as she felt comfortable around the town and confident in the tattoo artist he recommended, she would do just that and get it taken care of. In the interim, she wasn't going to wear anything that could show it. Jeremy felt responsible in some ways, but he shouldn't. He'd been there when the branding happened, but he couldn't blow his cover yet.

Then she thought about where Jeremy was taking her now. He feared that all the other places that were supposed to be safe wouldn't be. Or maybe they were, but she and Jeremy were so paranoid that they left those places and moved on. But she knew it was a burden to have her with him. He couldn't conduct an investigation worrying about her every five minutes. Mateo and Deavan had disappeared, and there was no sign of them anywhere. The feds were still collecting evidence and putting associates of Mateo behind bars. Some politicians got caught up in the arrests, as well as lawyers and other people that had a lot of pull. It was a major mess, and Jeremy was working to resolve it all.

The medication the doctors prescribed to help her sleep wasn't really working. She was scared, and feeling safe enough to relax and catch up on needed sleep just wasn't happening.

She exhaled as she looked in the mirror.

The bruises were long gone, but the feeling in her gut was strong as ever. It made her feel sick to think that Mateo had let Deavan have his way with her body. She really didn't know if he had or he hadn't. She prayed that he hadn't, and she knew she might never know the truth. It made her have such a deep fear she avoided being touched, even when Jeremy tried to take her hand or hold her close when she would fall asleep next to him on a long drive. He had saved her, and she owed him so much.

He'd blown his cover as an agent. The raid he'd organized failed because Mateo and Deavan were a few steps ahead and there was someone dirty working in the federal agency. Another reason they moved on from the known safe houses and were now headed to personal friends of Jeremy's.

She put on her bra, adjusting her extra large mounds into the small cups of the bra. She had always been well endowed. Voluptuous was an understatement with boobs like hers. They'd gotten her plenty of attention as a teen and even more in her twenties. It was a part of her body that made her feel self-conscious. She never flaunted her assets. She always tried hiding them. Except for in front of Mateo. If she wore a blouse, he would unbutton another button to reveal more. If she asked him what dress to wear to an event he wanted her to attend, he picked it out, and it was always sexier than her own taste. She had a traditional full figure, and she worked out very hard to make sure she didn't get loose and flabby.

She swallowed hard as she pulled on the T-shirt and then stepped into the shorts. She had never been weak-minded, yet so easily she allowed Mateo to mold her into the woman he wanted and expected. She had been so weak and stupid. If she ever got out of this mess and could have a normal life, she would be sure to hold onto her true identity and not allow the influence of others overpower her.

Her natural olive complexion made her stand out as well. But all she wanted to do was hide. She didn't want to leave the hotel. She didn't want to look at people and to feel inferior, ashamed, weak, and stand out as a victim. She wanted to be strong. She wanted to get through this and have a life. But with Mateo and Deavan still out there somewhere free, it just didn't seem like a real possibility.

She gasped when she heard the knock at the door and grabbed the vanity.

"Sophia, it's time to go. Are you okay?" Jeremy asked her.

"Yes. I'm coming now."

She gave one last look in the mirror, grabbed her brush and the other items that were already packed up. This was it. Another place, another hideout, but she wished it were the last. Sophia just wasn't sure how long she could keep going on like this.

* * * *

"Where are the others?" Nate asked Lew as they met outside of the small beach house.

"I figured from what you told me about the young woman, we shouldn't meet her all at once. Might intimidate her."

Nate smirked. "Yeah, that's a smart idea, but somehow I get the feeling she'll still be intimidated by four giants like you and your team," Nate said just as they heard the vehicle approaching. A black sedan with tinted windows pulled slowly up the long driveway.

They both stood there as the vehicle approached, parked, and then one guy in casual pants and a dress shirt got out. Lew didn't like the way he looked around the place or at them. He was glad that Nate took care of the greetings.

Then another guy got out. It had to be Jeremy. He spoke to someone in the vehicle while Nate introduced Lew to the first agent.

"This is Lew Masters. He and his team will be providing security and care for Miss Brown throughout her stay," Nate said.

The guy gave Lew the once-over.

"Read your file. Impressive. Here's a file on Miss Brown and her medical conditions."

"Medical conditions?" Lew asked, taking the file the agent handed to him.

"She's been through a traumatic experience and needs some sleep aids to cope. It's all in the file. We have contact numbers in there, all secure lines, in case medical assistance is necessary beyond what we've provided thus far."

He glanced at Jeremy, who reached in and helped someone out of the car.

The moment the young woman, Sophia Brown, stepped out of the car, Lew's eyes were glued to her. She was gorgeous and had a hell of a figure on her. Even the other agents watched her closely as she made her way toward them.

Jeremy and Nate embraced.

"Good to see you. Sorry it had to be on these terms," Jeremy said to Nate.

"Me too, Jay. Next time," Nate said.

"You've got it," Jeremy replied, and then Nate introduced Jeremy to Lew.

Lew gave him the once-over. The man kept eye contact with Lew, and Lew thought that was a good sign. The man didn't seem to be hiding anything, but he did keep a hand at Sophia's lower back. She looked nervous as her eyes darted to Lew and Nate then around the area and back to Jeremy.

"Sophia, I'm Nate, a good friend of Jay's."

She gave a soft, not quite authentic, smile.

"Hello, Nate, Jeremy told me all about you and your friends," she said in a shaky voice.

Then she looked at Lew, who had to give his head a little shake to get with the program. He'd seen plenty of women in his lifetime who were drop-dead gorgeous, but none of them compared to Sophia. This immediate attraction and protective feeling came over him, and that was not cool. Never had that happened.

"I'm Lew. I'll be watching over you for the duration of your stay," he told her as their eyes locked, and she lowered her head and turned away. She was more than shy. She was scared.

Jeremy placed his hand on her shoulder.

"Remember what I told you. You can trust Nate, Lew, and his team. The four of them live next door to the house you'll be staying in, and Nate, his brothers, and their woman live about ten minutes from here," Jeremy told her.

She swallowed hard and nodded.

"They have our secure contact numbers. I'm going to call you on that special phone I gave you to check in when I can."

"I'll be okay, Jeremy."

Jeremy held her gaze and then gave a soft, reassuring smile, and she just stared at him. Lew couldn't help the odd feelings he had. He wondered if there was something romantic between Jeremy and Sophia. Then he wondered why he'd even thought that and why it bothered him.

It was odd, but as Jeremy and the agents left, and it was him, Sophia and Nate alone, he could see how uncomfortable and fearful she really was.

"So, I guess the first thing we should do is show you around the place. Lew and his team have a beautiful beach house that's all yours. Their house is this one right here," Nate told her, and she looked at it.

"It's very big. I wouldn't expect to see so many trees. It's almost hidden," she replied in a soft tone.

"Well, wait until you see the back yard," Nate told her and winked.

"Well, let's start off here by the driveway," Lew said. "In the garage we have a series of vehicles. If you need to take one, we'll work out a schedule. Down this path leads directly to a walkway that leads to your house, as well as another entrance to the beach. However, we tend to use the back door to our porch."

"Jeremy mentioned that one of the local markets offers delivery service for food and things," she said as they began walking toward the pathway. Sophia picked up the large duffel bag, despite Nate's offer to carry it for her. She also had a backpack in purple on her shoulder.

"Shopping is only a short five minutes from here. You can use the car, or if it's just a few items, we have bikes," Lew suggested.

Then she looked at him. "I'll need that number for the delivery service please." Then she continued to walk down the path.

Lew looked at Nate, who seemed to read into that statement, too. Perhaps she was still living in fear and really didn't trust easily. It would take some time. But Lew was really interested in reading the file Jeremy had given him.

As they approached the dividing walkways between their house and Sophia's beach house, she stopped in her tracks. She seemed completely affected by the view, the gorgeous semi-private beach before her and the roar of the ocean as it hit the shoreline.

"Stunning, right? One of the best views in Treasure Town," Nate said, and then she cleared her throat and walked to the left.

* * * *

Sophia was speechless. Never in her life had she seen any place more beautiful than here. She couldn't help but to inhale deeply. The scent of ocean air filled her senses. She could imagine listening to the sound of the waves rolling into the shoreline as she lay in bed at night. The house was just as stunning as Lew's but smaller, and from where the deck stood, she could see his deck and what appeared to be a swimming pool.

"Your house doesn't have a swimming pool, but there is a hot tub under there. I'll come in once a week and make sure it's clean. The chemicals all up to level, so no need to worry about it. Just enjoy it," Lew told her, and she looked away from him.

The man was so big she could hardly stop the fearful shaking feeling in her gut. She didn't even want to speak and come across so intimidated. She didn't know these men. She didn't trust them, or anyone for that matter, and the sooner she established she wasn't socializing with anyone, the better.

"You have two entrances. One in the front of the house and this one on the back deck. We have a cleaning service that comes in every other week."

"I won't need that. I'll clean the house myself."

"Jeremy paid for that service."

"Credit him back. I can do it. I don't mind cleaning. I'll be fine," she said, and they entered the house.

She was shocked at how gorgeous it was. There were high windows everywhere and even a large indoor sitting room and balcony that looked out over the ocean and the glorious view. Was that a telescope set up there?

"Everything in the house is yours to use. There's another telescope in the closet on the upper deck toward the side of the house. But the one up there has a better vantage point," Lew said.

"I bet it does. This is really very nice. How come no one is renting it now?" she asked.

"My team and I didn't want just anyone renting it." He looked down at her, holding her gaze.

"It's a stunning place, and they had asked all of us to keep it in mind if someone was looking, so when Jeremy called, it was a no-brainer," Nate told her.

"I'm not sure."

"What are you not sure about?" Nate asked her.

She chewed her lower lip.

"Sophia, we want you to feel comfortable with us. I've known Jay, Jeremy, for years. Whatever you're thinking, or worried about, please don't hesitate to tell me or Lew and his team. We're here to help you get through this," Nate told her.

She looked at the two large men and then nodded.

"There's a whole beach out there, and ocean too, and anyone can come along from either place and sneak up in here."

Both men looked at her as if she were crazy, but she didn't care. They didn't know what had been done to her and how resourceful Mateo could be. Especially now on the run. He knew people.

"Honey, don't be afraid of anyone coming up to this place like that," Nate said. "We've got security covered. Besides, from what Jeremy explained, it seems that these men, who may or may not still be after you, are in hiding from the feds. No one except for Jeremy, the two agents he was with, and us know where you are. Lew and his team are retired Navy SEALs. The best of the best, and you can trust them."

She just couldn't shake the fear she had, but she wasn't about to argue with such intimidating men, so she dropped it. So much for enjoying a sound sleep and listening to the waves rolling in.

Twenty minutes later, Nate left, and Lew stood by the counter in the kitchen with a list of numbers and the keys to the house.

She stood a good distance away from him, intimidated by his size and by the way he looked at her as if he could read her mind. He explained about the AC and how it worked and about garbage and other minor things that seemed to be on the list in the folder, but she hardly heard any of it. She wondered how tall he was and why he seemed to favor his right shoulder and every so often would rub over his chest on that side. His jet-black hair was nearly to his shoulders, making him appear rugged and intense. She didn't want to stare at him, but his green eyes were quite striking and the muscles and hardness of his body, never mind his facial expressions, definitely affected her. Especially those thick chords of muscles that stood out on his neck as well as his forearms. The man was in excellent physical condition.

"Did you have any questions?" he asked her, and she shook her head.

"I'll figure things out."

He pulled out a cell phone and placed it onto the brown granite counter in the kitchen. Then he held her gaze with a very intense and serious expression.

"This is for you. You're to keep it on you or near you at all times. Just in case of an emergency or if you need assistance for anything you're not sure of or can't figure out. We are one phone call away. The four of us are your first four contacts. You just press one, and it speed dials us."

"I have the one Jeremy gave me."

He shook his head.

"That's for him to contact you. He's trying to find these men and will be working the field. Sometimes he'll be unreachable. My team and I are your first contacts and aids in any situation."

She swallowed hard. She looked down at the phone.

"I'm sure I'll be fine on my own."

"No. This isn't up for discussion. I believe Jeremy told you that you're to do as my team and I ask. That means full cooperation without second-guessing or hiding anything from us. We can't protect you if you don't let us in on what you may need. I don't care if you hear an odd sound during the night or something spooks you and you can't sleep. You're to call me or one of the others. Got it?"

Sophia wasn't certain she liked this guy one bit. He might be very attractive, have big muscles, and been a Navy SEAL, but his demanding tone and the scary way he looked at her were enough to make her cower. She looked away from him.

"Sophia."

She turned back. "I understand."

They held one another's gazes, and then he pushed the phone closer to her.

"Show me you know how to use it. Start it up."

He made her feel like a child. She could see that he had some years on her. Okay, maybe ten or so, but his condescending tone was not received nicely. She decided it was better to not argue and just give the man what he wanted. For now that was, until she could build up her physical and mental strength. She was still very down on herself and being negative.

She picked up the phone, opened up the phone keypad, and then looked at the list.

"I'm number one. You're to try me first because more often than not I'll be close by. Gideon is number 2. He will be working less hours for the marine patrol then Andreas, who is number three and Cerdic, who is number 4 on the auto dial. Got it?"

She nodded, and he raised both eyebrows at her. She understood he wanted her to test it. She pressed one and hit the button for speaker. Immediately the phone on his hip rang.

"Good. Press number 2."

"Now?"

He nodded, and she left it on speaker then hit number two. The moment the deep, intense voice answered, she couldn't speak. "Hello? Hello, Sophia?"

"We're testing the line. All is good. Later."

"Yes, sir."

She couldn't believe her body's reaction to the tone of voice of bodyguard number two, Gideon. Holy crap. He sounded like a man with a thick beard, who smoked cigars and set off bombs. It was deep, scrappy, and hard.

"Well?" Lew pushed, and she went on to test number 3 and then number four. After hearing each of their voices, she now was curious as to whether they looked like she thought they might because of their voices.

"You'll get to meet each of them in the next several days. Every couple of days we'll drop off a schedule of where we'll be and what may be going on so you'll know who your first contact should be if you need anything."

"Why don't you just text it to me?" she asked, already feeling on edge and very unsure about how this was going to work. They would constantly be around her, and she wasn't sure she wanted that. She was trying to pull her shit together and get stronger, and she didn't think being around strange men who looked like giants would be helpful.

"Sophia, we're here to protect you, and in doing so, we will be doing a house check and, at night, a perimeter check. We'll even do a beach check so you feel safe and secure. You'll get used to us being around, and you'll feel more comfortable. I promise."

She wondered if she would actually get comfortable or if their size and their attitudes would do the opposite and put her on edge. She truly wasn't sure, but it appeared she had no choice and was about to find out.

"We'll see," she said, and he crossed his arms in front of his chest. She stepped away from him farther.

"If there's nothing more, I'm pretty tired."

He stared at her.

"That's it for now. Just remember that phone goes everywhere with you. We'll talk later. Oh, and there are some basic things in the refrigerator and the cupboards to eat. We weren't sure what you liked, but until we get a list from you and get to the store tomorrow, it will help you for tonight."

She didn't argue and tell him she planned on ordering and having the groceries delivered. Earlier he hadn't seemed too keen on that.

He nodded and then headed out the door from the kitchen to the deck and down the pathway. She locked the door and then went through the entire house, making sure every window and door was locked. She felt sad because the air was beautiful, and a gentle breeze felt good filtering through the house. But feeling safe was more important, and she just didn't know if such a place existed, never mind if she would ever feel safe again.

Chapter 3

"I don't know what I was expecting but not for her to look like this. Not after the file we got from Jeremy prior to her arrival," Lew told his team as he passed around her picture.

Andreas whistled low. "My God, she's gorgeous. What the fuck was she doing with this asshole?" Andreas stared at her picture and then passed it to Cerdic.

"Damn," Cerdic replied and then passed it to Gideon.

"It's hard to believe, but however they got involved, it turned ugly fast," Lew said. "As you all could see going over the file, this guy Mateo is bad news with lots of connections and resources he is currently tapping in on. It's been months since Jeremy blew his cover and got her out of there. No sign of the prick or his partner, Deavan Hoyt. Although our part in this case is strictly to be bodyguards and protect Sophia, Jeremy has given us some access to some of the details surrounding the case and Sophia's part. As you all could see, the narcissistic bastard went as far as branding his employees and men that were loyal to his business organization. Jeremy has the mark on his upper arm."

"That's sick, never mind fucking painful. This guy Mateo is into other masochistic shit?" Gideon asked.

"From what I've read, he has some fetish with fire, burning people who have not exactly succeeded in pulling off his requested missions and deals. They have also connected him with a series of five missing people, all professional people from lawyers to a doctor. Somehow there's a connection between them and Mateo's business dealings. Not our problem, but it gives us an image of the kind of environment

Sophia was forced to remain in. Jeremy said she had no idea until recently that this guy was cheating on her, committing criminal acts, and when she found out, she demanded to leave. It didn't happen."

"What did he do to her, Lew?" Andreas asked.

"Not a clue and Jeremy didn't specify. He just said what she went through was traumatic and that she was going to need time to heal."

"So what's the next step?" Gideon asked, taking her picture into his hand and staring at it.

"Introducing yourselves and making her feel safe. She won't engage in much conversation. She'll try to blow off any need for help. Just give her the time she needs. Our job is safety and security. I think we can handle that."

* * * *

"What's the obsession about? We just barely got you out of the fucking country on that cargo plane, Mateo. Do you want to end up in prison for life, or do you want to live and never look back?" Castella Moya asked Mateo as Mateo declined another offer of a blowjob by some goddess of a whore Castella had walking around his estate. The man was a millionaire with connections across the globe.

Mateo looked at Deavan, who was smiling wide and caressing the ass of a woman who wore a purple string bikini. They were all sitting by the outdoor pool, the music played softly in the background, and Mateo and Castella were in the cabana. This place, Castella's home, was like something out of a movie. It was paradise. He was so glad that he'd started doing some business with him last year and that they had gotten close. Mateo got some of Castella's men out of prison quickly. He also hooked them up with drugs, booze, and women during the time they spent in jail waiting to be released.

Mateo didn't answer Castella. His thoughts were on Sophia and, of course, Jeremy. Castella had gotten copies of the surveillance videos at the hotel suite in Chicago. He saw how Jeremy got Sophia out of there and into an SUV with federal agents. It killed Mateo to think Jeremy was an agent working undercover and privy to so much information, information that could send Mateo to prison for life, but he worried more about what Sophia knew and what he'd sworn her to secrecy about. If she dared tell the feds about the safety deposit box and then bank accounts in Europe, his funds would be seized and he would be broke. In that safety deposit box was a key to another safe and documents, thumb drives, files with evidence of hits he'd done, fires he'd started, and people he'd killed to prove he was legit and could handle anything.

His actions had gained him respect and business deals. He was fucked if she told the feds about the security boxes. But then again, he wasn't certain she knew of them or even recalled him talking to Deavan about them that night he branded her and they played with her body. God, he missed her body, the feel of her large breasts and firm, round ass. Even the way she filled out her clothing from dresses to those short skirts and sexy bras and panties. *Fuck, I can't live without her. I can't.*

"Jesus, Mateo. This woman is that important to you? That fucking special you're willing to risk your location? I won't be part of this. I won't risk my estate, all I've fought for and worked so hard for here in Venezuela. You want to hire men to find her and bring her to you, then you do it away from here."

Mateo looked at Castella.

"This was only temporary, Castella. You know as well as I do that I would never place you in danger. I need a few more weeks. I need men to locate Sophia before I can make plans to get her delivered to me."

Castella took a puff from his cigar and exhaled. The smoke twirled around and then into the warm air.

"Then you need a place that will be too difficult to get to you. A place filled with dangers for any federal agents wanting to rescue her. Perhaps Cordoba?"

"Colombia? I don't know if that is good enough. Jeremy had to be highly trained, and federal agents these days seem to be comprised of retired soldiers. Men like that would find me too quickly."

"Then maybe Panama, one of the small villages. I know people. Or perhaps Ecuador or even Peru? It won't be exotic and beautiful, but in a year or two when the heat dies down, you can move with her closer to the water's edge. To the islands and tropical places you've loved."

"You are right, but I need to find her first, and considering our snitch is trying to secure his cover, it may take some time."

"You're very impatient, Mateo. But lucky for you, I have some connections of my own." Castella snapped his fingers, and one of the servants came over.

"Call Frederick Price and set up a secure conference call for me tonight with him."

Mateo nodded and thanked Castella.

Mateo thought about Sophia and her sexy, curvy body, the way her thick, long brown hair fell nearly to the middle of her back, and how obedient and faithful she was to him. If he had only been faithful to her, she never would have gone with Jeremy. Unless Jeremy had already been fucking her. Maybe they had an affair, and that was why she'd left with him. But how could he do the things he enjoyed in bed with other women with sweet, innocent Sophia? She had been a virgin, and he had her first and would be the only one to decide who fucked her and who didn't.

If she cheated on him with Jeremy, then he would torture both of them together. He couldn't hurt Sophia in the way his body, his sexual appetite needed to. When he'd branded her skin, seen her beautiful flesh part and turn red and bleed, it had aroused him entirely too much to analyze. If he did to her what he did to other women, burned them, left forever marks of his on their bodies, she would have died. As it was, he tended to take things too far. She needed to stay perfect and unharmed. The M branded on her lower back would forever be a reminder and a symbol of his ownership. It wouldn't matter if it took months or years to find her. He would, and when he did, he would make certain she knew the only way to leave him would be by his hands, taking her final breath.

* * * *

Sophia awoke in a panic. She gasped and jumped up, trying to familiarize herself with the new surroundings. The sound of the ocean could be heard outside, despite the closed windows. She calmed her breathing and felt the burning against her skin. The damn marking on her back. It ached as a constant reminder of her being Mateo's possession. Not anymore. One day she would remove it, hide it, or turn it into something beautiful, not ugly and evil.

She looked around the room, which was so big and filled with light. It was a stunning bedroom, a dream home altogether and hers for as long as Jeremy thought it was safe. When she thought about that, she thought about Lew and his team. She would meet them all today at some point, and she needed to get mentally ready.

She climbed out of bed and stretched her arms. A shower first and then she would need to look up information on the Internet about the shopping and home delivery service. From there she needed any clothing stores that might deliver, or she may be forced to head out. But not today. Not any time soon. Too risky. What if he were out there or one of his buddies? Then what? She felt the shiver of trepidation and fear. Would this ever go away?

After her shower, she headed downstairs, prepared to make some coffee and figure out the password for the Internet. She'd forgotten to get that from Lew, but as she turned the corner, she spotted a guy on her deck. She gasped. Where the hell is the phone? She thought about it a moment, and there it sat, right on the island where she'd left it last night. She was being stubborn. A second glance toward the door and she saw that he was cleaning the hot tub. Really? At this time of the morning? Then she looked at the microwave. Eleven? She should have known. She hadn't fallen to sleep until six and then kept waking up. The last time she looked at the clock it was nine. Two hours sleep? Not bad at all.

She held the phone and debated about calling. But Lew did say there were four of them, including him, around, and they took care of the house. She watched him closely. He was a big guy, almost as tall as Lew, at least six feet three, and filled with muscles. Then he bent over to grab some chemicals and, man, did he have a nice ass. As he stood up, he turned toward the sliders, and she gasped, pulled the phone to her ear, and hit the auto dial 1.

The guy was watching her but didn't move a muscle. In fact, he raised his hands up palms forward as if signifying he was harmless and wouldn't move a muscle.

"Sophia, what's wrong?" Lew asked in that hard, deep, angry voice of his.

"Uhm, there's a guy here. On the deck by the Jacuzzi."

Lew exhaled. "It's okay. That's Gideon. He's one of my team, and I sent him over there because I'm stuck fixing something at one of our rentals up the road."

"Are you sure it's him? What does he look like?" she asked, wanting to be a hundred percent sure.

"Six foot three, two hundred pounds, brown wavy hair, brown eyes, and an expression right now that makes him appear annoyed I'm sure."

"His hands are up."

"So that you know he's a good guy. Open the door and ask him his name while I'm on the phone."

She swallowed hard and slowly moved closer. Gideon, if that was him, gave her body the once-over. She probably shouldn't be wearing a tank dress. She slowly cracked the door open.

"Identify yourself," she said to him.

"Gideon Sparks, ma'am. One of Lew's team members and one of your bodyguards." He eyed her body over. She felt her cheeks warm, but she quickly closed the door and locked it. "Go ahead back to what you were doing," she said through the glass door.

"All good, Sophia?" Lew asked.

"Yes. Thank you."

She disconnected the call and then leaned against the counter, holding the phone to her chest. Gideon watched her and then placed his hands on his hips and gave her an annoyed expression. She could hear him through the glass doors.

"Unlock the door, Sophia." She didn't move.

He spoke as if he were ordering her around, just as Lew did.

"We need to meet so you won't get scared again," he said, and she thought about it a moment. She looked him over. He was bigger than big, especially compare to her. Not that she was a peanut, but these men, Gideon and Lew, made her feel like one.

He nodded toward the door, his expression again annoyed as she slowly unlocked the door and then pulled it slightly open.

He stared down into her eyes then at her lips.

"I'm Gideon. You'll be seeing a lot of me around here and the other two, Andreas and Cerdic. In fact, Andreas should be coming by soon to do a sweep of the house."

"That's not necessary."

"Well, you're not in charge. Lew is," he snapped at her, and she stepped back, suddenly afraid of this man Gideon, despite that fact that he was supposed to be a good guy.

He exhaled.

"Listen, we're here to do a job, to keep you safe and secure. Jeremy asked us to watch over you, and that's exactly what we're going to do and our way. Now, the Jacuzzi is all set and cleaned. The beach has been checked by Cerdic, so if you would like, you can go out to the beach while we do the house check."

She crossed her arms and stared up at him, wondering why he was so hard and abrupt, thinking how annoyed it made her but also how aroused she felt. It was crazy. He wasn't even her type at all. Not that she had a type. In fact, she needed to do some heavy soul searching while here so she could figure out what she wanted and needed in a man and whether that was even a possibility. As far as she knew, she was destined for loneliness and had a future of living in fear as long as Mateo and Deavan were on the loose.

She swallowed hard, as he seemed to look over her body again. She was well endowed and then some. Finding a bra to fit her big breasts was annoying, and having guys drool over her boobs was just as annoying.

"I won't be going to the beach. I'll stay here in the kitchen. Your sweep or whatever shouldn't take long. I haven't even been here a full twenty-four hours."

"I'm sure Andreas will be fine with that. So do you need help with finding your way around the kitchen?"

"I'm good," she said, and he nodded and then walked away.

She watched him pick up the bucket and supplies of chemicals and then head off the porch. He waved to someone, but from where she stood, even with her face practically pressed against the glass, she couldn't see who it was. Probably Andreas or Cerdic, as they called him. What interesting names. They sounded like the names cavemen had. That made her chuckle to herself as she looked around the cabinets for coffee after she spotted the maker on the counter.

She started to make a full pot, thinking she had a lot to do online to learn about Treasure Town and what it may or may not have to offer her. Jeremy had given her the name of a reputable tattoo parlor and a guy named Tank he knew very well. He also mentioned that if she wanted to get a job working somewhere that Nate and even Lew would help her out. She wasn't sure if she believed all Jeremy's hype about this town. Growing up in Chicago was way different than the beach and boardwalk life. It made her look at the number of the tattoo parlor again. She couldn't even lay out in a bikini and enjoy the sun and getting a tan. Not with Mateo's marking on her. She needed to get rid of it, or hide it somehow, but how could she trust this guy Tank? She didn't know if he was capable of doing such a thing. She didn't want to answer his questions or have him look at her as if she were some whore whose man claimed her by marking her permanently. She felt the tears fill her eyes and then heard a knock at the glass door.

She turned around as she gripped the counter behind her, and Lew was there with two other men, not Gideon, who she had just met. He looked concerned, and she lowered her head, wiped her eyes, and then made her way to the glass doors. She unlocked one and opened it.

"Are you okay? What's wrong?" He looked around the kitchen as if something specific had set her into tears.

"Nothing. I'm fine." stepped aside.

He looked at her eyes then lower before scanning the kitchen again and then behind him.

"Meet Cerdic and Andreas," he said to her.

Sophia felt her heart begin to race. These men were each bigger, sexier, than the next. Both wore camo shorts and had tight T-shirts on that showed off muscles upon muscles. The scent of men's cologne filtered through the kitchen. It smelled so good she found herself inhaling to get a better whiff.

"Sophia." Cerdic reached out to shake her hand.

When their hands touched, he squinted slightly but showed no other reaction, unlike her body, which completely found these men sexy as damn hell. She looked away from his dark eyes, and then Andreas reached his hand out.

"Andreas, nice to finally meet you.".

She felt just as strong an attraction to him as she did with the others. She knew this was bad. She shouldn't want anything to do with any men. Men hurt, manipulated, and took advantage of women.

She pulled back. "I guess you're all doing a sweep of the house as Gideon mentioned?" she asked and then headed over to the coffee maker.

"That's the plan. Then Andreas and Cerdic are headed to the store in town. Do you have a list or maybe you'd like to join them to see the town?" Lew suggested.

She stared at him, surprised at the offer. She would have loved to if things were normal, but things weren't. She was scared that Mateo was around and could spot her at any moment. She wasn't even sure about getting to the tattoo artist's place. She had a lot to figure out.

She shook her head. "I'll call it in and order. I also need the password for the Wi-Fi."

"If you go online, limit your searches. Don't look up anything having to do with the case, with your ex, or even Jeremy. Strictly use the Internet to make your shopping list, look around at the town, and basic stuff. Got it?" He gave her a stern expression.

One look at the other two men, and she wouldn't dare venture from Lew's command. She nodded.

He walked closer to her, took the pen and pad on the counter, and wrote down the password for the Wi-Fi. "If you have any problems, let me know. Next week one of us can drive you into town for any food or things you might need. It's safe here, Sophia." Lew then headed deeper into the kitchen.

Andreas, with his dirty blond hair and brown eyes, watched her. Cerdic had his arms crossed in front of his chest and was looking down at her, even from a few feet away. God, they were big.

"Okay, Cerdic upstairs, Andreas, downstairs. I've got the perimeter," Lew said to them, and they nodded and then took off after the order was given.

It was so wild, and the fact that Lew showed so much authority and the men responded with respect like military men would made her feel a slight bit of relief. Were they really going to be able to protect her? Would Mateo find her? She didn't know the answers, but like

Jeremy had told her, she needed to move on and start making a new life. He felt that Treasure Town was the place to do it.

* * * *

Cerdic looked at Andreas as they waited in the driveway for Lew.

"What did you think of her?" Cerdic asked.

Andreas raised one of his eyebrows.

"She seemed okay, like not too scared."

"Probably because she met Gideon this morning and he told her about us all coming by. What else did you notice?" Cerdic asked.

"I know what you're asking, and she was not what I expected. I don't know. Maybe I thought she would be like some damsel in distress, I don't know."

"Well, I sure as shit didn't expect to see the emotion in her eyes, the glossiness from tears about to shed, and feel concerned like Lew obviously did. I could sense his anger toward the situation and her being scared like that, despite knowing we're the good guys. His back stiffened, and he looked ready to kill. You know, that facial expression he gets when someone is hurting and they're an innocent."

"Hell, I just met her, and I was on the defensive, too. The woman is incredibly attractive. I mean that long thick brown hair and dark blue eyes were fucking hard not to stare at."

"Yeah, and as the eyes went lower, the view got even better."

Cerdic chuckled.

"Shit."

"What's going on, all good?" Lew asked.

Cerdic looked at Andreas.

"How under guard does she have to be?" Cerdic asked.

"What do you mean?"

"He means she's very attractive, and she stands out in a lot of ways. How much freedom is she allowed? Do we follow her when or if she goes anywhere?" Andreas asked.

"Mostly it will be my job to watch over her like that. But I want her comfortable with all of us. From what Jeremy and Nate explained, she's scared and probably won't go anywhere for a while. Once we help her see that we're here to watch over her, just in case, then she might loosen up and head out to town. One day at a time. I don't want this to interfere with your jobs. I know you've made a commitment to the marine patrol."

"You're not doing this on your own. We'll work it out together. Besides, we're kind of new in Treasure Town, too. It's been years, and things have changed. We could learn about it together, and that could help ease her into trusting us. Then she'll be more comfortable," Cerdic suggested. Andreas chuckled.

"We have a job to do. Getting personally involved with her is not a smart idea. Be nice but that's it. Keeping her safe and remaining diligent and on guard is a must. Got it?" Lew stated firmly.

"Got it," Cerdic and Andreas replied together, and then they headed back to their house.

Chapter 4

"So what are you telling me? They want to drop the case, forget the investigation, and let off on these men? They killed six federal agents, multiple lawyers, a doctor, and God knows who else. They're out there. It's just a matter of time," Jeremy said to his supervisor and the head of the task force the agency had established.

"Jeremy, it's been six months. We have men now working undercover in Scaggs' operation. He seems to have taken over where Mateo had been. The guys up top want to take this operation down, not hunt the previous leader," special agent of operations, Jack Banks, told him.

Jeremy ran his fingers through his hair.

"And what about me? My cover's been blown, and the one witness to his acts, and a victim in all this, is Sophia. Are you giving up on us, saying we're on our own?"

"Of course not. This isn't over yet. They are willing to give a little more time. But it could be weeks, not months."

"Wonderful. Mateo and Deavan are alive. They will be back, they will strike again, and they will come after Sophia and me."

"You've ensured her safety, and no one but you and the two agents you've been working with know her whereabouts. Keep it that way and she'll be safe. Have her move on with her life. Mateo is not going to risk going to jail for life to come back to the States to get this woman."

"First of all, you don't know Mateo Ruiz the way that I do. He will come back for her. She is his property, and he will kill her by his own hands before he lets another man have her. And as far as him being out of the country, nothing has been confirmed, just as we still have not figured out who the snitch in this operation is."

"Now that is your explanation for a raid gone to shit and you blowing your cover. There's no evidence to prove that our agency, this special operations team, has a rat in it."

Jeremy stood up and paced.

"Are you really that fucking dense, or are you telling me that someone up top wants this investigation to end so badly that they're willing to let Mateo go free?"

Jack Banks stared at him.

"I'll keep you posted on the time frame. It's out of my hands. Unless Mateo shows up and attempts to kill you or this ex-girlfriend, and basically falls into our laps, I can't see this ending any other way then running out of time. I'm sorry."

"Sure you are, Banks. Sure you are." Jeremy walked out of the room.

He wanted to fucking hit somebody, but as he scanned the room, he caught only three people watching him. One of them he really didn't know. He was new to the agency as far as Jeremy knew. Maybe it was wiser to focus on who the snitch could be instead of finding Mateo. He could be out of the country. But the snitch was still around, keeping watch and hoping to find out where Sophia was. Jeremy needed to be very careful. He might have to call in his brothers for assistance.

* * * *

Two weeks had passed, and Sophia decided that she would sit out on the beach where no one else was while the men did their weekly sweep of her house and offered to take her into town. She might as well take them up on it since Jeremy had called and so much had changed. He sounded defeated. It wasn't looking good. It seemed the agency didn't really care as much about finding Mateo as they did about nailing Scaggs, who seemed to be the new leader of Mateo's business operations. Jeremy also mentioned her moving on with her life, maybe finding work because the agency probably wouldn't foot the bill for her living arrangements.

She found the information unnerving and was surprised at the disappointed feeling in her gut. She was getting used to the men walking around watching over her, and she had even conversed with Lew and Cerdic a few times. She was starting to understand why they were so hard and commanding. She looked up what she could on Navy SEALs and discovered they were definitely resourceful men who risked their lives and even went through intense training in water and on land. It was commendable. She figured that was why they had so many muscles and that led to her thinking about her poor choice in a first boyfriend and lover and how that choice had nearly killed her and ultimately ruined her life.

But Jeremy's words played in her head. A reminder that she had an opportunity to rebuild herself and her life, or she could just sit here, be scared, feel sorry for herself, and give up. Instead, she wanted to be stronger. When she thought about getting stronger, she thought about physically wanting to better herself besides mentally. She thought about Lew and how she watched him at night on the beach. She could only see him when the moonlight was bright, but he would do these martial arts moves, in slow motion and then faster, but ultimately it looked therapeutic. He did favor that left side of his, but with all those muscles, and his arms and legs moving so perfectly, it made her want to ask him more about it.

She exhaled and then looked at her watch. She wondered if the men were at her house doing the sweep yet. She anticipated asking them to take her to town, and she wondered if Jeremy had talked to them about the possibility of her having to pay for the house she rented from them. She needed to know how much rent was, and that would help her to see how many hours she would need to work and doing what kind of job.

She stood up, looked out toward the water, and thought it was a stunning setting. When she turned to look toward the house, she gasped as Lew approached.

She quickly, pulled the shirt from the chair, and tried to get it right side out. She didn't want him to see her back, but it was too late. She had been facing the water. The tears filled her eyes as panic set in. He would think terrible things of her. This was why she didn't sit out here unless she knew they wouldn't be around. But one look at his expression as she locked gazes, and she knew he'd seen the damage to her skin.

"Oh God, you scared me." She fumbled with the shirt. He was by her immediately.

"Sophia, what is that on your back?" he asked and took her arm and turned her.

She pulled from his hold. "Nothing. What are you doing?" she asked, getting angry. God, she didn't want him to see it and to know that Mateo had marked her forever as his woman in such a barbaric fashion.

He stared at her, and she saw him lick his lower lip.

"Sophia." He continued to hold on to her arm. Something moved in the distance. One look past Lew and she saw Cerdic coming down now, too.

As Cerdic approached, his eyes roamed over her breasts then to her waist and legs. He was checking her out, and she felt the tears fill her eyes.

She looked up into Lew's eyes.

"Please don't," she whispered to Lew. He swallowed hard and released her arm as she quickly pulled the shirt up and over her head.

"Sorry, I didn't mean to scare you. The guys are in the house now. I was wondering if you needed anything? I know you've basically said no every day, but I still wanted to ask," Cerdic said to her, sounding hopeful she would say yes this time.

"Uhm, actually, I was thinking about checking out the town. I have a few errands to run. Maybe you could give me directions and I could take one of the bikes?"

She started to gather the towel and the chair she had set up down in the sand.

"No, we'll drive you and accompany you to wherever you need to go," Lew said rather abruptly.

She didn't want to make eye contact with him. She knew this conversation about what he might have seen was not going to be over. If he took her to the store, then he would ask her about it.

"But that won't be necessary. I know you have things to do with the other houses," she said to him.

"Not at all. Until you feel safe and know your way around town, it would be better for at least one of us to be nearby. When will you be ready?"

Feeling safe seemed impossible. How could she feel safe and even make an attempt at starting over when this damn mark on her body repressed her in every aspect, especially in feeling safe or even trusting?

"I just need to change and wash up. I won't be long, if you're sure."

"We're sure," Cerdic said, making it obvious that he intended on coming along, too.

Great. She was going to be around both of them. Could she do this? She wasn't sure, but they wouldn't let her go to town alone. Not yet and she really wanted to check it out, as well as the tattoo shop. There didn't seem to be another way.

* * * *

Lew and Cerdic waited outside by the truck.

"What's up with you? You're pissed off about something," Cerdic said to him.

Lew released a long sigh and looked at the house and then at Cerdic.

"When I went down to the beach to talk to Sophia, I saw something?"

"What? Someone on the beach?"

Lew shook his head.

"I'm pretty sure it was some kind of marking on her lower back, but then she freaked out, reached for her shirt, and my eyes went right to the fearful expression on her face, and I knew she was upset that I'd seen whatever it was."

"A tattoo maybe?"

"No."

Sophia opened the door, closed it, and then headed toward them. She wore a pale beige skirt, a light tank top in black, and carried her purple backpack. Her hair was pulled back into a ponytail, and she looked gorgeous. Lew felt guilty for seeing something on her body that she obviously wanted to hide. He wanted to know what it was and why she was so upset that he'd seen it. But instead, he opened the driver's side door as Cerdic opened the passenger door, let her get in before him, and they headed out to town together.

* * * *

The ride was quick, and after Lew told Cerdic about the marking on Sophia's back, he found himself wondering what it was. But they walked her through town and had pointed out various places when they spotted Nate, Rye, Mike, and Turbo Hawkins, along with their girlfriend, Frankie.

They greeted them and immediately Nate introduced Frankie to Sophia. Cerdic kept close to her on one side, and Lew was flanking Sophia's other side.

"It's nice to meet you, Sophia."

"Same here," Sophia said and then smiled at Nate.

"She's renting the beach house Lew and his team own. How do you like it, Sophia?" Nate asked.

"Oh, it's beautiful."

"I heard that it has amazing views and a great private beach. You're so lucky," Frankie told her.

"The beach is very private and really nice. I was on it for the first time today."

"Glad to hear that you like it," Nate said.

"Hey, we're going to Sullivan's for lunch. Would you three like to join us?" Frankie asked.

Cerdic looked at Sophia, who looked at Lew, and Cerdic couldn't help the emotions he felt. She sought out the commander's response and permission to reply. It was submissive, obedient, and somehow turned Cerdic on to her femininity and sweetness. He felt overwhelmed, but then Sophia spoke up.

"I needed to do a few things, but if you tell me where the place is, I could meet you guys and your friends there," she said to Lew.

"We're not heading there for another fifteen minutes or so. We can save three more seats for you guys. Take your time," Nate said to them, and they nodded and then walked away.

"If you don't feel comfortable, we don't have to meet them," Lew told her.

"I just don't think it would be wise to make friends here. I don't know how long I'll be around, and it will just hurt more and make it harder. It's how we handled the other places where we hid."

Cerdic was angry and truly felt badly for her. It wasn't fair that she had to live a life of fear and go from place to place because of these men who were after her.

"This may very well be the place you get to start over and begin a new life. Making friends can help. You should remain positive that Jeremy will find the men who want to hurt you," Lew said to her, and as he placed his hand at her lower back, she jumped and shuddered from his touch.

She looked scared as she stepped away. "I'm fine, really. I guess you may be right about making friends, and maybe Jeremy will be able to solve the case. It couldn't hurt to look into the possibility of finding work."

"Finding work? Why?" Cerdic asked.

"Because when I heard from Jeremy, it sounded like the government might cut the ties from us and leave us with no means of financial assistance. I would have to work and probably leave your house and find something very small to start."

"No. That won't be necessary. You can stay in the house for as long as you want. We'll help you."

"But I can't promise that I could ever replay you," she whispered.

"It's not necessary," Lew said. "We're your first friends in Treasure Town, and we won't be the last ones you make. Now let's go do those errands, meet up with the guys and Frankie, and then hit the grocery store before heading home."

She nodded, and they walked down the street.

Cerdic was shocked at what he was thinking and feeling. He wanted to learn more about Sophia. He wanted to make her feel safe and have the new start she deserved, but something told him that getting her to let her guard down would be hell. He even wondered if he could keep his promise about not getting personally involved with Sophia. Maybe Lew and the others would find it too difficult, too.

* * * *

Sophia was surprised at how comfortable she felt around Frankie and all the men. Frankie had an outgoing personality, and before they'd finished lunch, she told Sophia if she ever wanted company shopping or doing errands that she could pick her up and take her into town or even meet for lunch.

"The girls get together at least a couple a times a month for ladies night out or even a day excursion. Manicures, pedicures, boutique shopping, a movie, a boat ride, whatever we plan. In fact, Friday we're going to a wine tasting event, where you learn to paint a portrait from instructors while tasting wine and eating gourmet food. It should be pretty funny. Sometimes some of the ladies drink too much and we get hysterical over the finished artwork."

"She's not kidding, and she's brought home some doozies," Hal teased, and Frankie gave him a light slap against his arm.

"Hal!" she reprimanded, and the guys all laughed.

One glance at Lew and Cerdic and Sophia saw something flash in their eyes, and then they looked so serious.

"You should come with me. I'm the designated driver this time around so my artwork should be superb. Thank you," Frankie said sarcastically.

Hal pulled her close and whispered into her ear as he kissed his woman. Sophia watched and could see the love, the bond, between Frankie and her men. Even the big bad sheriff, who intimidated Sophia big time, smiled and gave Frankie a sweet wink.

Frankie looked at Sophia, waiting for an answer.

"Oh, I'll see. I'm not sure," Sophia replied.

Cerdic placed his arm over her chair. The move not only made Sophia freeze. The table grew very quiet. Frankie's eyes widened, and Jake, the sheriff, Hal, Hank, and Nate all watched with interested expressions.

"You can go if you want to," he whispered close to her ear. "It might be nice to make some friends so you feel more comfortable here."

Her heart pounded, and her breasts felt fuller, aroused by Cerdic's close proximity, his heated breath, and sexy, caring tone.

She didn't look at him. Instead she looked down at her lap.

"I'll think about it."

"Good. We'll exchange numbers and keep in touch. It's only a few days away. You'll have a blast, and the women are all really sweet," Frankie told her, and then they started talking about a place called the Station and how they would all meet up there for beers while the women were out Friday night.

Sophia thought about how normal and happy they all seemed. Even these ménage relationships were so acceptable and common, and they truly seemed happy, loved, and cared for. Frankie's men were definitely protective, too, and in a good way not an abusive way. Watching them in action with Frankie made Sophia understand the difference and realize, even more so, what her relationship with Mateo had lacked. Trust, commitment, and, mostly, respect.

* * * *

Throughout lunch, Cerdic watched Sophia's reaction to their friends and to Frankie. She really seemed to hit it off with Frankie, and he thought that was great. But as she excused herself to go to the lady's room, and Cerdic saw multiple men checking Sophia out, he couldn't believe the jealous, protective feeling he had. It was instant, and it shocked him. But one glance at Lew and Cerdic saw that he looked so serious with his eyes glued to Sophia, and then he gave a near snarl at the men who blatantly watched her.

Frankie got up to take a phone call so Cerdic and Lew were left with the guys.

"So, how are things really going? *Is* she getting more comfortable?" Nate asked.

"Well, she's been with us for a couple of weeks now, and today is the first time she's allowed us to take her into town. She wants to come in alone, but I'm not sure that's a good idea," Lew said with his gaze bouncing toward the group of three men who had watched Sophia walk to the lady's room.

Jake looked over his shoulder.

"Why is that?" Nate asked.

"Just want to be sure she's protected," Lew replied.

"Or maybe you don't like the fact that other men are looking at her, and you guys are attracted to Sophia," Jake said.

Cerdic kept a straight face.

"We're just doing the job you and Jeremy asked us to do," Lew replied.

"Doesn't look that way to us, but hey, stranger things have happened. It's not like she's some criminal," Hal added.

"No, she isn't, but she's been through hell, and she needs time to recover. She sure doesn't need four non-commitment-type SEALs fucking with her head," Nate said very seriously.

Cerdic sat forward, his temper getting the better of him.

"What the fuck do you think, Nate? That we would take advantage of her?" Cerdic asked.

"Who said we're the non-commitment types? You haven't even seen us in years. You don't know what type of men we are, what type of team," Lew said, very seriously but calmly. Cerdic knew that tone. If this little argument went further, fists might fly.

Nate looked at Jake, and Jake nodded his head and smiled as he leaned back in his chair. He crossed his arms in front of his chest.

"So, are Gideon and Andreas attracted to her too?" Jake asked.

Nate snorted as he shook his head.

"Holy shit, who would have fucking known the four of you badass SEALs would wind up robbing the cradle big time?"

The other guys laughed, and then Cerdic exhaled and leaned back in his chair. Lew, however, retorted right back.

"My understanding is that Frankie is a good ten years younger than you, old man, so I wouldn't talk," Lew stated, and Cerdic chuckled.

"Ten years is one thing, but last I checked, Sophia was twenty-three, and you're thirty-six," Jake replied, and they all chuckled.

"Hey, all kidding aside, what's your plan of action?" Nate asked. "I mean she's not out of danger. Jeremy could show up and whisk her away if these men who are after her come too close. She was hurt pretty badly from my understanding."

Lew exhaled, and Cerdic watched the door waiting for Sophia to come out. Frankie headed that way, too, after her phone call.

"I get the feeling," Lew said and then glanced at Cerdic before continuing, "that she was abused by this guy. Today on the beach, I kind of snuck up on her. I thought she would have sensed me coming closer, but she was so lost in thought, looking out at the ocean, that when she turned around toward the house, she gasped and grabbed her cover up. I saw something on her back. I tried to see what it was, but she freaked, and tears filled her eyes. There was something there."

Cerdic swallowed hard.

"Bruising and injury?" Jake asked. Now he looked just as angry as the others did with his eyes wide and his arms crossed in front of his chest. All these men had complete respect for women and were protective of all. Of course they would show concern and be upset over this.

"Nothing was in the file Jeremy gave you guys?" Jake asked, and Lew shook his head and leaned back.

Nate exhaled. He looked around them.

"I know what it has to be. But, fuck, I hoped it hadn't been what Jeremy meant when he said she'd suffered and he couldn't take not getting Sophia out of there," Nate said.

"What? What do you mean?" Cerdic asked.

"You read about this fucking guy. He branded his men, anyone close to him." Nate then looked away, exhaling and running a hand through his hair. At first Cerdic wasn't sure what he meant, and then it hit him like it hit Lew, Jake, Hal, and the others.

"He branded her? Burned her with a prong like she was some object, a possession?" Lew asked, teeth clenched.

"Oh fuck, no." Hal blew out a long breath.

Lew's eyes popped up, and then Cerdic saw Sophia and Frankie coming from the bathroom.

"They're coming back," Hal said.

Cerdic watched the men flirt with Sophia and Frankie. One stood up from the stool, and Cerdic and Lew were standing up in a flash that alerted the others, who all stood, too. But before they moved, Frankie pointed at the guys, saying something as she looped her arm through Sophia's and then pointed to Cerdic and Lew and the others. The men immediately placed their hands in the air and sat back down, but their gazes roamed over the women's asses.

"Sit down, we're fine," Frankie said, letting go of Sophia's arm.

Cerdic moved so she could sit, and he couldn't help but to touch her arm.

"Okay?" he asked, and she nodded, and they all sat back down. Everyone was quiet.

"So, Sophia, you really should consider going out with Frankie and the girls Friday. It will be fun, and the place is right outside of Treasure Town."

"Say yes, Sophia. I promise it will be fun," Frankie told her, and Sophia looked at Cerdic and at Lew.

Cerdic gave her a nod and a reassuring smile as he kept his arm over her chair behind her shoulders.

"Okay, I guess so, if Cerdic and Lew say it's okay."

Cerdic felt his chest tighten. Was she beginning to trust them and their judgment, their indication and promise that she was safe here in Treasure Town? He wasn't certain, but he sure knew he liked her looking to him and Lew for reassurance and for their permission. He wondered if she were a natural submissive, or if her ex was so controlling and demanding, abusive, that she'd had no choice. As much as a submissive woman tuned him on, he would rather have Sophia handing over control to him because she trusted him, felt the connection, and wanted to, not because she felt she had to. Seemed to Cerdic that they sure did have a lot to figure out, but at least Lew seemed to admit he was attracted to Sophia, too. So maybe their rule of not getting involved would be broken.

* * * *

"Is there someplace else you wanted to go before we head back to the house?" Lew asked Sophia as she carried her bags of groceries and placed them into the back of the truck. Cerdic carried theirs and placed them inside.

"I think I'm good for today. I'll probably take one of the bikes out Thursday and come here to go to the clothing store. I really don't have a lot of things, and I'll need something for Friday and then, of course, if I get any job interviews, I'll need clothes, too."

"Andreas and Gideon can always bring you. They're off Thursday and Friday."

"I don't know how long I'll be. I wouldn't want to hold them up." She stepped back when Lew touched her hand. She froze in place, and he stared down into her dark blue eyes.

"It's not a problem. We like spending time with you. Don't you like spending time with us?" he asked, and then he couldn't resist. He reached up and pressed a stray hair behind her ear, her skin smooth against his palm.

She went to say something and then closed her mouth. He held her chin and tilted it up toward him as Cerdic came to stand right next to her. Her eyes darted from Lew's to Cerdic's and back again.

"Well, don't you like spending time with all of us?" Cerdic pushed.

"Yes," she whispered softly.

Lew gave a soft grin. "Good, then it's settled. Andreas and Gideon will drive you into town Thursday. How about we get this stuff home and you come over for dinner tonight?"

But before she could answer, his cell phone rang. He gave her a wink, and they all got into the truck as Lew spoke to one of the tenants about a broken garbage disposal.

"Looks like I'll be cooking the steaks on the grill tonight," Cerdic teased, and they all headed back to the house.

* * * *

Sophia didn't think she could handle this dinner with the four intimidating men. She thought it wasn't a smart idea for so many reasons as she looked in the mirror and pressed her hand down the beige skirt before she readjusted her breasts in the pale blue sleeveless blouse she wore. She wondered if she should undo another button. That was what Mateo would have wanted her to do, but it wasn't her taste. She hated flaunting her breasts. She left two undone and only because she would be busting out of the top if she didn't and wouldn't be comfortable. She took a deep breath.

This isn't a date, so why am I so nervous?

But the way Lew looked down into her eyes and asked her about dinner and feeling comfortable with them and liking to spend time with them swirled around in her head. She was attracted to all four men. Their friends were all involved with ménage relationships, and the men were definitely attracted to her, but how could she follow her heart or let down her guard when danger was imminent?

Mateo would kill them if she got romantically involved with these four men. It wasn't fair to them to place them in such danger. She felt the ache to her back. Although the branding looked more like a strange tattoo now, and was no longer raised and painful looking, she still knew what it stood for. She was Mateo's possession, an object he owned and controlled, even now that he was gone on the run. But she knew him so well. He would return. Even if it took months or years he would do it.

The tear escaped from her eye, and she quickly wiped it away. How would Cerdic, Andreas, Gideon, and Lew react when they saw the branding? It was one thing to have sexual relationships with men and have lovers, boyfriends. But it was different, sick and despicable and degrading to be branded by one so no other man would touch her, want her, or respect her. That was what hurt the most. Perhaps her future entailed sexual partners to ease a need for a connection and some form of compassion and affection, but ultimately she would be alone, considered used, damaged goods that no one would want but for sex.

The tears flowed, and she felt sick to her stomach. She couldn't go over there and pretend she was a normal woman with a normal body, a normal heart, and normal past. She was anything but normal. A battered, scarred victim, a woman destined to be alone and never truly loved.

She walked over to the bed and opened the container of prescription Valium the doctor had prescribed to help calm her nerves and help her to relax. The tears continued to flow, and she took a pill then drank the water. She climbed up onto the bed and cried her heart out. Thoughts of no future and always living in fear had her sniffling and moaning until exhaustion overtook her.

* * * *

"She isn't answering. I'm going over," Andreas said, and he put the cell phone back into the clip on his waist.

"We all are. Something might be wrong," Lew added, and the four of them headed next door.

They made their way through the house as if they were in a raid, guns drawn, securing each room from bottom to top floor. Andreas's heart was pounding for he feared she was hurt and somehow someone had gotten into the house and taken her. He thought about the conversation he and Gideon had with Lew and Cerdic about their admittance to being attracted to Sophia as well and wanting to pursue the feelings but knowing she was fearful and a victim of violence by a man who she thought had loved her. But then, as they got to her bedroom and his eyes landed on her back, the branding they feared she'd sustained in plain sight, his stomach pulled into knots. They placed their guns into their holsters, and Lew picked up the prescription bottle.

"She took Valium."

Gideon sat down on the bed and caressed her hair from her cheek.

"Looks like she's been crying." Andreas couldn't help the upset he felt and then the anger as he stared at her beautiful skin and then the letter M so bold and bright against her lower back.

"I hope she didn't take more than one," Cerdic said, and then it became a panic to wake her. How unstable was she? Could she try to take her life? What had possessed her to lie here and take the pills?

"Sophia? Sophia baby, wake up now. It's Gideon," he said to her as he caressed her cheek.

They all sighed in relief as she exhaled and then slowly opened her eyes.

"Gideon?" she whispered and then rolled to her back and stretched. The move accentuated her large breasts. Her skirt lifted, and more sexy thigh showed. Then she gasped.

"Oh God." She went to sit up, and then she grabbed onto Gideon.

"Easy, baby. Take your time. I think you took some Valium."

"How many did you take?" Lew demanded to know.

Her eyes widened. "One," she whispered, and then she seemed to catch sight of their guns and the fact that they were all in her bedroom. She reached up to make sure her blouse wasn't undone, but her breasts were so big, so beautiful, that they flowed from the top.

She was gorgeous, Andreas thought as he sat down on the bed.

"What's wrong? Why the guns? Is he coming? Did he find me?" she asked, looking panicked as she gripped the comforter, her eyes wide with fear.

"Shhh, no, baby, we just got worried that you didn't come over. We were waiting for you," Andreas said and then reached up and caressed her cheek.

She lowered her eyes.

"What happened? Why did you take the pill when we were expecting you to come over?" Lew barked at her, putting Andreas on guard. Even Andreas and Cerdic were shocked as they looked at Lew with strange expressions and then to Sophia.

"I'm sorry, Lew."

"Why?" he pushed. "Were you considering doing something to hurt yourself?"

She shook her head.

"Were you in pain?" Andreas asked as he caressed along her back.

She pulled away.

"You saw it?" she asked, voice quivering.

Andreas swallowed hard and nodded.

She covered her face. "That's why." She started to cry.

"Sweetie, what is it? What do you mean?" he asked as he caressed her hair and then her shoulders.

Gideon was up on the bed, kneeling and caressing her back.

"You didn't want us to see it, did you? And you were afraid that we would tonight because of the attraction we feel," Lew said to her.

She uncovered her face and held his gaze.

"The fact that he did that to you just makes us want him dead even more. He had no right to force that mark on you and try to claim you like some object."

"But he did, and I am. I'll always belong to Mateo," she said.

He shook his head as Andreas said, "No, baby, no way." Andreas caressed her cheek and tilted her chin up toward him.

"He's gone, and we'll make sure he never lays a hand on you again."

The tears rolled down her cheeks.

"But you won't be able to. He'll kill you to get to me. He'll kill anyone who tries to take what belongs to him." She said it with such fear and emotion that Andreas could tell that she believed that mark was more than skin deep.

"No, you are not his," Lew said. "You never were, and some mark forced on your skin against your will does not signify an eternal bond and ownership. Unless you stand here and tell us you love him and that you want to belong to him and will be his forever, then that's different."

"No. No, I don't want that. I hate him. I hate what he did to me. I hate feeling like shit, like a nobody that no one will ever love or respect. I don't, Lew, I swear," she cried out.

Lew stepped closer and knelt on the bed as Andreas stood up to get out of the way. Lew pressed between her thighs, cupped her face, and tilted it up toward him. He held her gaze, his fingers gentle against her throat and chin in such a deep, sensual manner Andreas felt the sincerity and the connection even as a bystander watching.

"Then you are free to become ours. To let down that wall, the fear, and allow us in. Allow us to care for you and to show you how real men treat their woman. Let us show you, Sophia. We want you, and that branding doesn't mean a damn thing."

He lowered his mouth to hers and kissed her softly. He was gentle, passionate, caring, and slow in his show of desire and affection for her. When he saw her reach up and gently glide her hands along his forearms, Andreas felt relieved, positive, and encouraged that Sophia was their special woman, the one to fill their hearts and connect them in the ultimate way they'd only fantasized about.

* * * *

Sophia was lost in the kiss and in the emotion and powerful proclamation Lew had made to her before he kissed her so tenderly. Never had she felt so aroused and like the center of a man's complete attention. As he lowered her to the bed, pressed between her thighs and deepened the kiss, she let him. It wasn't until he released her lips and held himself above her that she remembered the audience and the fact that four, extra large men were in her bedroom, armed, and appearing aroused and hungry.

She took uneasy breaths, her chest rising and falling, his eyes roaming over her cleavage and then back to her lips. Obviously the Valium had calmed her fears and nerves because, otherwise, she would be running for the nearest hideaway and covering her head in embarrassment and fear.

"Easy, baby, just relax. We're not going to hurt you or overwhelm you," Lew said, and then Andreas reached out and caressed her chin. He gave a soft smile.

"You're so sweet, so beautiful, you deserve the world," he said.

"Are you okay?" Lew asked her, and she looked at him and then at Gideon and Cerdic.

"I think so, thanks to the Valium."

Lew squinted and stood up. He reached for her and helped her into a sitting position.

"You don't need to take that stuff. Not in fear of us, of this attraction, it isn't necessary and could become addictive."

She heard the intensity in his tone and the expression on his chiseled, muscular face reiterated the fact that he meant business.

"You don't need that shit to get better and stronger mentally and physically."

It sounded like he knew first-hand. Had he had a drug addiction at some time and was he assuming she was heading in that direction?

"I'm not addicted. I only take a half a Valium some nights when the nightmares are bad. But you sound like you had a personal bad experience."

He placed his hands on his hips, and one rested on the butt of the gun on his waist. She swallowed hard. She had four bodyguards that were ready to shoot and kill anyone who tried to break in and take her. It brought realty back mighty fast.

"We've all had injuries in the military where we needed narcotics to deal for several days or weeks. We've seen friends become addicted, and then it led to other drugs. We don't want to see the pain in your past make the wrong decisions for your future," Gideon told her.

She smoothed out her skirt and ran her hand along her jaw.

"Sometimes the nightmares are just too painful, that's all."

"You can't sleep without the pills the doctor gave you?" Cerdic asked and then took a seat next to her on the bed.

She shook her head. "Like you said, I don't want to become addicted so, instead, I only sleep a few hours maybe a night."

"That explains why you're so tired all the time and how exhausted you were today when we were in town," Cerdic replied.

"But you weren't going to sleep now. You were supposed to come over to dinner. What happened?" Lew asked.

She was quiet. She didn't want to explain her fears. They could use them against her. But as quickly as she had that thought, she realized they weren't like that. At least she didn't believe them to be.

She clasped her hands on her lap and stared at her fingers. Then Cerdic covered them with his hand.

"Were you thinking about him and what he did to you?"

She nodded.

"What else made you cry and get so upset that you felt the need to take the Valium?" Andreas asked next.

These men were so in tune to her emotions, and it was as if they really cared and wanted to be here for her. She'd let Lew kiss her. He told her they all wanted her to be theirs. She needed to let them know her fears and what she was thinking so that they knew she needed slow.

"Sophia?" Cerdic said.

"I was thinking about the four of you and these feelings I have. I don't have a right to feel them, to be attracted to you because I could never belong to you."

"Why not?" Lew asked in that deep, hard tone of his.

"Because of the mark. Because Mateo said I belonged to him and only him and that he would kill anyone who tried to take me from him."

They hissed in anger.

"That's not true. It's a mark. It was forced upon you and means nothing because he no longer means anything," Gideon told her.

"It may seem so easy to you, to tell me it means nothing and to forget about it and move on, but I can't."

"Do you still love him, want to forgive him?" Cerdic asked her. and she shook her head.

"That night, I wanted to leave him. I knew he'd cheated on me, and his behavior toward me was disrespectful. When I told him, he struck me in front of a crowd of people. That night he branded me in front of Jeremy and Deavan, his right-hand man."

"Bastard," Cerdic stated firmly.

She thought about the pain and about the drugs Mateo had given her and how she'd woken up being touched by Deavan. She didn't know if he raped her. How could she allow these men so close?

She stood up and wrapped her arms around herself as she kept her back to them.

"Sophia, what is it? What are you not telling us?" Gideon asked.

She stared out the window and the evening sky over the ocean. The stars were bright, and there was promise out there, but not for her.

"I don't think I can get involved with the four of you."

"Why not?" Lew asked.

She didn't respond, and then she felt the hand on her elbow.

"Why not, Sophia? Tell us now why you can't give into this attraction and let us in," Lew demanded to know.

The tears filled her eyes.

"Because that night Mateo branded my skin he drugged me because I was in so much pain. When I woke up, I was naked in bed, and he and Deavan were touching me. I don't remember anything. I don't know if they raped me, and when I tried saying no and pushing Deavan's hands away, he touched me intimately anyway, and there was nothing I could do. Mateo let him," she told them as tears streamed down her cheeks.

"Those fucking pieces of shit," Cerdic stated loudly, and Lew pulled her into his arms and hugged her tightly.

He shocked her as he caressed her back and held her close. "I'm so sorry, baby. So sorry they did that to you. No wonder you've stayed inside and wouldn't go anywhere. We're going to take good care of you. None of what they did matters to us. You were a victim. They're the criminal monsters, and we would never hurt you, ever."

She wanted to believe Lew. She wanted to feel beautiful and loved, but she just wasn't sure she could. But then as she hugged him back, and he squeezed her close and kissed the top of her head, and then the others caressed her and kissed her shoulder, her head, she felt overwhelmed with emotion. They kissed her everywhere, and then, someone lifted her shirt and pressed their lips against the scar on her lower back.

She lost it. She sniffled and cried.

"Let go and let us take care of you and show you how beautiful you are and perfect," Lew said, and she let her arms fall to her sides as all four men continued to scatter kisses against her skin.

Lew stepped to the side, and Cerdic was there to caress her cheeks and tilt her chin up toward him before he kissed her gingerly. Her heart soared with adoration and desire. She'd never felt so aroused and cared for, and then he released her lips and Gideon took his place. He cupped her cheeks and kissed her chin, her nose, her eyelids and then her lips.

"You're perfect and so sexy. I can't wait to make you mine. To show you how beautiful and amazing you are." He kissed her again and then released her to Andreas.

Andreas gave her a wink and then pulled his bottom lip between his teeth, looking sexy. "This connection we share is special, and I want you to know that I've never felt this way before. So instantly in tune to a woman, so adamant about making you mine and knowing that no other men but my brothers and I will have you, will possess you. I know you'll need time, and you'll need slow," he said and gave her one sexy, devious smirk as he let his eyes roam over her breasts then to her lips.

"With you, I'm going to enjoy slow. Real slow," he said and then plunged his tongue between her lips and kissed her so deeply, with such vigor, that she didn't think that slow was possible with these emotions. In fact, slow might be highly over rated and might never happen.

* * * *

Andreas pulled out a chair for Sophia to sit at the dinner table. He gave her shoulders a squeeze, and they all gathered around to enjoy a nice dinner together. No one spoke of what had occurred earlier, and Andreas was fine with that. In the back of his mind, he thought about all the ways he would like to torture and kill the two men who had hurt her so badly. A few exchanged glances between his team, his brothers in arms, and he could tell they had her story on their minds.

He tried to focus on the conversation Gideon started about Sophia going out with Frankie and her friends and the positives of making new friends. He, however, thought about the potential danger, and he really wished they were involved in the investigative aspect of this situation. But one glance at Sophia and her sweet angelic face, those big blue eyes, and, of course, her sexy, full figure and he would be sure to take the position of her bodyguard over the limit.

"I would like to, I guess. I mean I should find some sort of job to make some money. It sounded like Jeremy wasn't sure about whether the investigation and search to find Mateo and Deavan would continue much longer," she said softly and then took a bite of steak off her fork.

"Jeremy wasn't certain about that." Lew stated.

Cerdic mumbled in agreement and then held her gaze.

"I think finding a job and keeping busy, making some new friends and getting used to Treasure Town is a good idea. However, we still need to take precautions. That phone Lew gave you must be on you at all times."

"I understand that. It will take some time to get used to going off on my own, but the town does seems nice, and so many people know one another."

"It is a great town. That's why we decided to retire here after Lew got out on injury," Gideon said.

Lew cleared his throat and gave Gideon a dirty look, and Gideon shrugged.

"You were injured while serving?" Sophia asked.

"Not a big deal." He kept eating.

"Sure as shit was a big deal. It's not every day you're nearly taken out by a sniper then held prisoner and left to die," Cerdic added in annoyance.

"Oh my God, you were shot and held prisoner? In like a prison camp? Where? Was it your shoulder or chest?" Sophia asked as she dropped her fork and stared at him.

"What? Why would you say my shoulder or chest?" he asked.

"You favor it. I've seen you stretch it out like it gets stiff or sore," Sophia told Lew, and he just stared at her.

"My chest."

"You could have died," she whispered and reached over and covered his hand with hers.

He pulled away and stood up. "No, no way, it wasn't a big deal." He walked away to get something in the kitchen.

She looked at the others, and Andreas gave her a sympathetic expression, knowing that Lew didn't like talking about getting shot. He thought by leaving the room, the subject would be dropped. If Lew pulled away from her like that, how would he expect Sophia to open up to him, or them?

Andreas reached over, took her hand, and brought it to his lips. He kissed her knuckles. "Finish eating. Then we can go onto the deck. It's a perfect night for star gazing."

She gave a small smile and then continued eating.

* * * *

As they cleaned up from dinner, the men took every opportunity to touch her, caress her skin, kiss her shoulder or her lips, and she felt so overwhelmed with desire. For the first time in a while her pussy clenched and spasmed with cream, and her heart raced with attraction for these four men. It was so wild. But as the night went on and they talked more and more, she felt as though anything was possible. She enjoyed their company. She liked feeling the center of attention and their desire. She needed it, craved the care and the need to touch. She felt desperate for anything they would give her, and that scared her, too.

So when Lew joined them on the deck and finally came up behind her and wrapped her in his arms, she relaxed and just allowed herself to feel.

He kissed her neck and her shoulder. She felt his hand move up over her ribs then to her breast.

She turned in his arms, and he held her gaze but kept stroking her breast, her nipple with his thumb. She shivered with desire, and neither said a word, but she touched him, too. She ran her palms up his chest, and when her hand went over the left side, he tightened instinctively.

He pinched her nipple through the blouse. She gasped.

"Feel good?" he whispered. She nodded.

"How about you?" she asked and caressed her palm up and down the left side of his chest then leaned forward. Then she kissed the entire area because she was unsure where the scar exactly was.

He lowered his lips to her cheeks, then lower, in search of her lips and kissed her deeply. He pressed her against the railing and ran his hands along her curves. She lifted her thigh as his palm caressed up higher to her panties, and then his fingers stroked down the crack of her ass. She pulled back and gasped for breath, and so did Lew. His expression was priceless, filled with so much hunger and need she felt faint. So badly she wanted to give into the sensations and let her body be taken by him, but in doing so, it would be exposed to the possibility of pain. They would make love to her together, and they would want to be inside of her together. She didn't want them to see that "M." She remembered Deavan's words as he said her lower back above her ass was a great place to brand her so that when they fucked her together they could look at it and know she belonged to Mateo and him.

She stepped back and tried to calm her breathing.

"Sophia?" Lew said and reached for her. She took his hand and brought it to her chest. She hugged his hand and held it tightly then looked at him and the others.

"I need time. There are things I need to do. I'm not ready to take the chance. I should head back to the house. Thank you for dinner."

He leaned forward and kissed her cheek. The others did the same, except for Gideon, who took her hand and said he would walk her back.

She hadn't wanted to leave or to stop the sensations Lew made her feel, but she couldn't give in and make love to them as long as this sign was on her body and she felt so unable to take care of things herself. Starting tomorrow she was going to make some changes and get her life back. She was going to go out with Frankie, make some friends, and land a job. If she'd learned one thing, she'd learned that, in order to open her heart and love others, she would first need to love herself.

Chapter 5

Sophia Brown closed her eyes as the buzzing of the needle continued to stain her skin. She took nice, easy breaths, her focus solely on getting rid of the damaged flesh she had been forced to live with for the last six months. She exhaled and tried to do the breathing exercises she'd read about online in order to keep the flashbacks at bay. It was crazy what was available on the Internet.

But it was too hard to forget. Too difficult to tamp down the need for closure. There were no bodies. No actual evidence to prove that Mateo and Deavan were dead. Instead, she would have to live with the fear that they were still alive and would seek revenge against the federal agents who'd destroyed their business, brought them down, and made her disappear.

She had no choice. She'd lost her loyalty to Mateo the moment he cheated on her, never mind branded her skin as a show of ownership and control over her life. She remembered that day, as clear as anything, especially the pain.

She cringed as the tattoo needle went over the more delicate part of the scarring. *This tattoo artist better be as good as Jeremy had said.* She was pissed off that she needed to turn the branded mark, the scar against her skin, into a tramp stamp on her lower back. But the marking was degrading and repulsive, reminding her of a time when she had no control over her life and nothing to look forward to but death. Things were different now. The design she'd picked began under her breast line, scattered along her ribs and around her hipbone, then even lower to her groin and over her hip to her lower back. It was so intricate that it had taken seven separate sessions to complete the masterpiece. But she wanted it done. She wanted to be able to sunbathe and enjoy the fact that she now lived near the beach, worked for a real estate company, and was finally doing well on her own. It was a hell of a lot better than where she'd been eight months ago.

She thought about Cerdic, Andreas, Gideon, and, of course, Lew. Damn Lew and his ultra-commanding, in-charge ways. Just because he'd been his men's commander in the Navy SEALs didn't mean he was in charge of her. She tried to ignore them, but who was she kidding? They were the four sexiest men she had ever laid eyes on, and here she was, still suppressing that attraction, still pushing them away. She even lied, and said she didn't have the same feelings for them they seemed to have for her. Lies, all lies to protect her heart and to move on with her life without the control and manipulation a man would have over her mind, body, and soul.

Mateo had screwed her up so badly with the abuse, the cheating, and the lies. And, then, to actually brand her with a metal letter *M* as a show of ownership and possession was sick. He didn't love her like she'd thought she loved him. She was nothing. She was also lucky that Jeremy had turned out to be working undercover instead of truly being Mateo's top leader in his gang of shit. That had been a shocker, but he'd saved her from getting raped. Or maybe he hadn't. Maybe she had been so drugged up from what Mateo and Deavan had given her after branding her that she didn't remember. She might never know, but assuming the worst made giving her body to another man impossible. *To four? No freaking way.*

She wasn't out of trouble yet. She might never truly be free from Mateo unless he and Deavan were dead. Until that day, and until she had concrete proof they were both dead, she would remain on her own, holding onto the evidence she had in her head. She would never step foot in Chicago, the city that had nearly killed her.

"About twenty minutes more, sugar. You holding up okay?" Tank asked her.

"All good. How is it looking?"

"You can't see the *M* anymore, sweets, and by the time I'm finished, you won't be able to find it yourself. Just remember, I asked for a full-body picture of this tattoo."

"I remember, and I'll do it for you. So don't worry."

"Ah, another plus to tattooing one sexy, fine piece like you."

She chuckled low. Tank had been hitting on her since day one, but that was just his style. For a guy as big and bulky as he was—with his burly hair and beard, tattoos, and a mean expression—he had the softest, most delicate touch. But she would never forget his artistic talent and his calm, sweet understanding when she'd showed him what she needed to get rid of. He understood.

"Focus, Tank. I'm hoping to be in the sun by next week."

"You will be, and maybe you can pick a nice stretch of beach down the block from here, specifically where I take my lunch? That way I get to see this sexy, curvy body of yours in a string bikini," he said. The buzzing sound continued, and her skin ached and burned.

"I doubt it. Hey, I thought you were kind of seeing that cute redhead that's always showing up with drinks for you."

"Cindy? Ahh, she's cute and all, but kind of young. Besides, she's really scared of Hector."

"Of Hector? Why? He's so nice," she said about his brother. One thing she learned about living in Treasure Town was that there were a lot of ménage relationships. In fact, she had become friendly with some of the women involved in such relationships, and they were thrilled. Some of them knew Lew and his team because of their friends. In fact, she was going to meet Frankie and go bikini-shopping this Friday.

"I don't know, but she needs to get over that fear if we're ever going to work out dating her."

"Oh, so you're into the whole sharing thing too, huh?"

"You sound disgusted with the idea."

"Me? No, not so much disgusted as I am uninterested, for me at least."

"Why is that? I've seen the men that hit on you. Hell, just yesterday while you were waiting for me to get started, Brooks and his buddy were asking you out."

"I know. I'm not interested."

He was quiet for a moment.

"Just out of curiosity, is it because of whatever happened to you and how you got this mark on your body, or is it just you're more traditional when it comes to men and dating one at a time?"

She took a deep breath and exhaled.

"Honestly, I think it would be different if I were normal."

"Normal? What's not fucking normal about you? I mean, besides the fact you have a hell of a fucking body and the biggest—"

"Tank!"

He cleared his throat. She knew he was going to say breasts. She wasn't exactly petite, except for her feet, a size five. Her ass was big too, but she had an hourglass figure, and sometimes, in today's fashion, having tits and ass of any decent size seemed unattractive. She'd never found skin and bones attractive.

"You know what I mean. You're fucking gorgeous, have an amazing body, gorgeous dark blue eyes, luscious lips, and are so sweet and smart. If a couple of guys, brothers, close friends wanted to commit to you and share you, provide for you, and take care of you in every sense, why would you not jump at the opportunity? Is it because of society?" he asked. She wondered if he wanted to know because he was thinking about Cindy, hoping she would come around and accept his brother Hector.

"Like I started to say, if I were normal, the bad things that happened to me had never happened, and two men—who were kind, caring, and truly into me—wanted to share me, make me theirs, and commit to me entirely, then yes. I would consider it. I've learned the hard way that life is just too short to not take chances, to do things your heart says are right, even if other people around you say they're wrong. I would do anything to feel safe and secure. To be loved by one man, never mind multiple, in that way. But I'm not someone who is capable of doing that. Not after everything that's happened. Not now, anyway. I'm just taking every day, one at a time."

"Damn, Sophia, I wish I could strangle the fuckers that hurt you. Who knows? Maybe it will just take the right man or men to prove to you that you deserve to be loved."

She swallowed hard. This was a deep conversation to be having with her new tattoo artist friend. But Tank was so easy to talk to.

"So what will you do about Cindy? Maybe ask Hector to be a little bit calmer and approachable with her and try to get to know her, too?"

"I don't know. I've tried talking to him. He's had some problems in the past. Got into some trouble a few years back. He paid for it. Served six months in jail. But I think it makes him feel like he isn't good enough. I don't know."

She exhaled and completely understood Hector's thinking. When she looked at Cerdic, Andreas, Gideon, and Lew, she thought the same thing, especially when other women flirted with them or checked them out. How could she open up her heart—her body—to four men and take such a chance, especially when she didn't even know if two men had raped her that night? To not remember a thing, only bits and pieces in her nightmares, didn't prove anything. In fact, it made her fear worse. She saw images of their hands, their fingers, touching her, trying to arouse her body, but she'd been in so much pain, and then the drugs made her lose her mind.

The tears filled her eyes, and then Tank whispered, "It's all done, sweetness, and I must say—you need to show this baby off. It's my best work ever."

He pulled over the mirror and then helped her to sit up.

She pushed her shorts to the top of her panties and then down on one side of her other thigh so she could look at the full tattoo. Lifting up her shirt to the cup of her breast, she stared at the flowering cherry blossom. As she squinted and looked closely, Tank appeared with a smaller mirror. He moved it so she could see and not have to let go of her clothing.

"Can you see the *M*?" he asked.

She stared at the tattoo, precisely where the *M* had been, but it had now turned into this intricate, beautiful design where no one could ever see the terrible, abusive act again.

"It's gone," she whispered as the tears filled her eyes and slowly leaked down her cheeks.

He squeezed her shoulder and smiled.

"Sure is, gorgeous. If this doesn't get you to move on with your life and open up your heart, I'm not sure what will."

She nodded and then wiped her eyes.

"Grab your camera, Tank. I'm ready."

He smiled, and then she adjusted her clothes slightly as he set up his camera, prepared to take some photos.

Until I was broken, I didn't know what I was made of. I've spent these last months thinking about all the wrong in my life and how I survived but also keep thinking about the fears in knowing they're still out there and could come for me at any time. But I can't live my life this way. I can't let the past dictate my future. It's time to rebuild myself. This time, I'm going to be stronger. I survived it all, and this is my second chance at life.

* * * *

"I found her," Gideon stated into the cell phone.

Lew had gone by the realty office where she had been working part time and they said she had the day off. She hadn't told them. In fact, she had been distancing herself from them since the night they all kissed and things got a little wild. Of course her days were busy, as she had started working for the real estate agency in town and handled all the bookkeeping as well as organizing vacation rentals. She was exhausted when she got home.

"Where?" Lew stated into the cell phone.

"The tattoo parlor. The one where people can watch tattoo artists working. Wait, I think she's coming out. Should I appear or what?"

"No, we'll talk to her about it tonight," Lew said and ended the call.

Gideon watched her walk down the street toward the deli, and she was smiling. Then he spotted Frankie, Serefina, and Michaela. They were obviously meeting for lunch, and as they hugged Sophia hello, he felt happy for her for making some friends. But then his heart ached and the fear that she couldn't love them or accept them as her lovers, her men, tugged at his heart. He'd never felt like this, and he wondered what more he and the guys could do to make her see that she was indeed special and could trust them with her heart and her soul?

* * * *

Sophia finished taking a shower. She applied some special lotion and looked at her new tattoo. She was overwhelmed with emotion every time she stared at the cherry blossom design. Tank had performed a miracle. Seven days, four-hour sessions, a few fibs about her work schedule to the guys, and she'd done it. The additional week letting the tattoo heal had been hell. One look at Gideon and she felt as though she had hurt his feelings. What had they expected? For her to just let them take her to bed and that all would be forgotten from her past? It wasn't that easy. In fact she felt the last few weeks had definitely been needed. She had learned a lot about ménage relationship from her new friends and gained a better understanding of what a commitment this would be if she decided to accept their advances.

She pulled on the deep blue sundress that zipped up the side over her tattoo and was too snug to wear a bra with. Then she heard the cell phone buzzing.

Quickly she looked at it and saw it was Jeremy. She smiled as she answered the call.

"Hi."

"Hey, how are you?"

She sat down in the chair that overlooked the deck and the ocean down below.

"Doing very well. Adjusting, working, making some friends." She heard him inhale and then slowly release a breath.

"Jeremy, is everything okay? Is there an update?" she asked.

"I'm sorry, Sophia, but the feds put a stop on the search for Mateo and Deavan. They seem to be satisfied enough to nail Scaggs and a crew of low-level thieves."

She felt the tears fill her eyes, and her heart began to race. "Where does that leave you and me?"

"Don't worry about me. It's you I want safe. I spoke with Nate and then Lew earlier. Lew said you're doing well and making some money. He said you can stay there as long as you want and that they wouldn't want you to leave. Sounds like you've become important to them and not just a job."

She sniffled. She couldn't help it.

"I don't know about that. I mean they're amazing men and they are a lot older and more experienced, but I'm not sure I'll ever be able to let my guard down, especially not now."

"I understand that you feel that way, but you're making a life for yourself. It could very well be that Mateo is out of the country and will remain in hiding for a long time."

"But there's always that worry he might come out of hiding and find me. As we both know, Mateo was always steps ahead and always had a plan. Why do you think he was able to botch that raid and disappear?"

"But you can't live your life that way. What Lew, Andreas, Cerdic, and Gideon want to offer you is special. There's no need to be alone anymore."

"I'll see what happens. When will I see you again?"

"To be honest, some things have changed for me, too. I can't let this go and allow Mateo, Deavan, and their crew of murderous assholes to get away with this. I've called in some help, people I trust, and without getting into any details with you, I think we're onto the rat, but the corruption runs deep. Keep close to your men. Let them care for you, protect you, and let them into your heart so they can love you. They've gone through hell in their lives, their careers, and are survivors, too. It's probably part of the attraction you all share. Go for it, Sophia. Treasure Town is a very special place."

"So I won't see you again?"

"Oh, I wouldn't say that. I have to see four Navy SEALs the size of those guys taking care of you, all mushy and lovey-dovey with you. That has got to be a sight."

"Nice, Jeremy. I'll be sure to tell them you said that."

"Good. Because I promise to deliver the news that Mateo and Deavan have been caught or are dead in person to you. Now take care and I'll be in touch."

"Stay safe, Jeremy."

"Give those men a chance, Sophia."

She smiled and then disconnected the call.

She looked out toward the sunset. The sun appeared to disappear into the water. She loved it here. She felt comfortable in this town and around the people, her new friends, and with her new job, hell, her new life. Could she stay? Could she let herself go and give in to the desires, the attraction she had to Lew and the others?

Immediately her heart said yes, and her body shivered with anticipation.

She stood up, looked at herself in the mirror, and then headed downstairs. As she came down the stairs, she heard the voices and then saw Andreas leaning on the shelf. They were all there, drinking beers and opening up a bottle of wine.

"What's going on in here?" she asked, and they all stood up straight and stared at her.

It was crazy, but there seemed to be this imaginary force surrounding them, a line, a connection, and as their eyes roamed over her body and the light, snug-fitting sundress she wore, she felt every part of her react. Her nipples hardened to tiny buds, and she knew they could see it through the thin material of the dress considering she was braless. Her legs shook, her pussy clenched, and she tried to walk deeper into the kitchen in a casual, carefree manner. But her heart pounded furiously, especially as she locked gazes with Cerdic. He licked his lower lip as he took in the sight of her. She turned away. It was too much.

"We need to talk." Lew stated firmly, his arms crossed in front of his wide, muscular chest, the black shirt he wore stretched to capacity. He looked incredibly handsome and was dressed casually, yet every ounce of her read his expression as dominant, hard, controlling, untrusting, and she gulped.

"Yes, Lew?"

It got so silent she could have heard a pin drop. The sexual charge in the room was choking her resolve to go slowly, to let them take their time touching her, but she was also renewed. She felt a rebirth of sorts just because the tattoo had made Mateo's branding, possessive mark disappear forever. She wanted to move on. She wanted to trust, to explore these feelings, and to feel more of their touches, caresses, and even their control.

When Lew held her gaze so firmly, and the cream dripped from her cunt, she knew things were not going to go as planned.

"You've been lying to us." Andreas desecrated the silence with that deep, hard tone of his as he took position beside Lew.

She felt guilty initially, but as Cerdic moved in behind her and Gideon too, she felt only aroused.

"Lied?" she asked.

Cerdic placed his hands on her hips, and she gasped, closed her eyes, and relished the feel of such large, manly hands on her hipbones.

She wanted to press her ass back, to feel his much-bigger body encase hers. She wanted to feel safe, comforted, cared for in every way, and she truly believed these men could do that. Even if it were only temporary.

That thought nearly brought tears to her eyes. She was shocked as her focus went to Lew. Cerdic walked her closer to their leader.

"I'm only going to ask you this once. We can't protect you, watch over you, be what you need if you're going to lie to us. You haven't been working extra hours. Gideon stopped by to see you today, and they said you weren't working. Where have you been going? Why couldn't you confide in us, trust us, Sophia? We don't know what more we can do to prove to you that we're real, we're staying, we want you in every way."

She saw the emotion, the anger, the insult in those gorgeous green eyes of his. One glace at Andreas and Gideon and she knew they were insulted and hurt too. But how could she explain why she had been pushing them away and why she needed to do this tattoo on her own and not let them see it? Until now that was.

"Sophia?" Andreas raised his voice, and boy, did her pussy react.

Jesus, why did she think making these men angry would lead to very enjoyable punishments? She could just imagine Lew, Andreas, and even Gideon tossing her over their knee and spanking her ass. Cerdic she wasn't certain of, but something told her he was filled with surprises.

Cerdic, at that moment, gripped her hips and gave her a light shake. His mouth landed on her shoulder, his lips pressed to her ear.

"Answer him, or they'll be hell to pay."

Holy. Freaking. Cow.

This was it. A moment of risk. But after what she had been through, this would hopefully only lead to better things and a real life, not one on the run and in constant fear.

"I'll need to show you." She went to step away, but Cerdic gripped her tighter. He ran his hand along her waist and over her belly.

"The truth, Sophia. We care about you so much. We want you in every way, but you can't keep pushing us away, torturing us. It just isn't fair."

She swallowed hard. "Let me show you, Cerdic. Please," she whispered, and he slowly released her, his touch so effective that the heavy feel of his large hand left remnants of warmth in their path.

She stepped to the right, and they surrounded her. So big and tall, intimidating to think that she was going to let them make love to her. Together, no holding back, no barriers, just letting go and allowing her heart, her desires, to lead the way. Whatever tomorrow brought, so be it. Tonight, she wanted to continue on the path to be healed.

"I'm sorry I lied. I'm sorry I've pushed each of you away. That night Lew kissed me and then things got a little wild, I realized what was holding me back from letting you into my heart, into my body."

They all gave her their full attention. That buzz of arousal, of connection, of desire flowed in and out, between their bodies and all around them.

"I couldn't move on, take the chance of letting you touch me, make love to me until I did everything I could to get rid of Mateo's touch."

"Don't say his name. Don't bring him up when he doesn't stand between us. He means nothing. His mark means nothing at all," Gideon said very fiercely, and she loved him for that. She softly smiled.

"It did to me, Gideon." His eyes widened. "But not anymore."

She reached under her arm and slowly began to unzip her dress. She pushed her hair aside and let the material fall as she held the material against her breasts just barely. She turned sideways and saw their expressions. It was Cerdic who fell to his knees and spread the material farther to her lower back where the M no longer could be seen.

"Sophia, my God, this is beautiful. It's gone," he said, and then the others came closer. They touched the design, they looked for the M, and they couldn't see it. She knew that, even if they could, they wouldn't say so. They understood, and she felt the tears fill her eyes.

Lew cupped her cheeks between his hands and tilted her head up toward him. He looked so powerful, in charge and dominant. She needed that. She wanted their control, their protective personalities and their bodies surrounding her.

"It's beautiful. Are you happy, Sophia?"

She was shocked as all her emotions flooded her heart. Her desire to have these men be physically part of her ruled her every thought.

"Not yet," she whispered and felt all their hands on her. Cerdic's fingers traced the cherry blossom tattoo. Gideon caressed her shoulders, and Andreas held her arm.

"What else will make you happy?" Lew asked.

She took an unsteady breath. "Belonging to the four of you," she said and released her hold on the material, letting it fall to the floor at her feet.

"Sweet Jesus, Sophia," Andreas whispered.

"Finally," Lew whispered as he kissed her deeply and their hands began to explore her body.

It was wild, more wild and arousing than she could have ever imagined.

Lew devoured her moans as Cerdic pressed her panties down and suckled her inner thigh. Andreas cupped her breast, and a moment later, she felt his teeth, his tongue, and then mouth feast on her.

Gideon squeezed her ass and pressed up against her as he suckled her neck.

"You're already ours Sophia. God, this body is made for us. Let us make love to you now, tonight." Lew released her lips and cupped her breasts.

"Yes. Yes." She hissed as Lew pulled on her nipple. Cerdic stroked her pussy with his tongue, and she pressed her ass back against Gideon. His hands gripped her ass cheeks, and he pumped against her ass.

"Let's get her upstairs so we can spread her out and really get a look at this body," Andreas said.

In a flash, they all pulled back, and Lew lifted her up into his arms. She wrapped her arm around his shoulder and neck and held his gaze.

"Let go with us. We want all of you, together."

She knew what he meant, and she was more than ready to explore this and be part of a ménage with them. She wanted what her new friends had. She wanted a life, a future, and she felt desperate to have it all with them.

"Protection?" Andreas asked as he stripped off his clothing. Those sexy, deep muscles and mega-hard thighs both aroused her and scared her. He could crush her.

"I'm on birth control," she whispered, knowing she had the IUD. She gasped as Gideon squeezed her ass cheeks and suckled her neck from behind.

"Oh God."

"I love this ass. I've been watching it for so long. I'm going to fuck this ass tonight, Sophia," he told her just as Cerdic fell to his knees, lifted her thigh up over his shoulder, and plunged his tongue into her cunt.

She moaned and leaned back against Gideon, who thrust against her ass, his cock covered by boxers, his bare chest pressed against her back. She felt feminine.

Cerdic replaced his tongue with a finger. He stroked her over and over again, and she came, she flowed, and thrust her hips forward.

"You're a fucking goddess, Sophia. Your body is perfect. You're perfect for us," Lew said to her, and as she locked gazes with him, he was stroking his cock, standing there naked in all his delicious glory. Then she saw the scar on his chest, and he pressed closer and kissed her. She gripped his hair and kissed him back.

When he released her lips, she ran her palm over the scar. "Lew?" she whispered, and he shook his head.

"I survived so I could be here with you and my brothers and make you ours."

She moaned just as she felt Cerdic pull his fingers from her cunt and Gideon stroke his fingers into her pussy from behind and then back over her anus. He did this repeatedly, and the thought of him taking her there had her shaking and spilling more cream.

"Gideon."

She moaned, and he pressed a finger against her anus and pushed in. Cerdic took that moment to press fingers to her cunt. All the while Lew stroked his cock and Andreas sat on the edge of the bed, naked and stroking his cock.

"Now. We need her now," Andreas stated firmly, and they pulled their fingers from her body. Gideon lifted her up and placed her onto Andreas.

He gripped her hips. "Ride me, baby. Make me yours."

She lowered her mouth to his and kissed him. She relished the feel of Andreas's hands massaging, squeezing her ass cheeks, widening them so hard that she ached and more cream dripped. She imagined Gideon taking her ass, and considering she'd never had anal sex before, she wanted to, so very badly.

Just at that moment, she lifted up, and Andreas gripped his cock until she sank down onto his shaft thinking, knowing, that sex never felt like this. Anything in the past was nothing compared to this.

She rocked her hips and then felt the hand at her back and a cock tap against her hip. Hands massaged along her tattoo and then lips kissed along the path of the design.

"So fucking sexy and gorgeous, just like you, Sophia. Great choice," Gideon told her, and then he licked along her anus back and forth, lubricating the entrance.

"Oh." She moaned with pleasure. Her breasts felt full, her nipples hard, and the bed dipped as Andreas cupped her one breast and pumped his hips upward as Cerdic licked the nipple Andreas offered him. She felt their hunger and the desire to claim her combined with her desire to claim them.

"I need that mouth. We're taking you together because this is how it will always be. We're one, and the bond can't ever be broken," Cerdic said to her and tugged on her nipple.

She creamed some more, and Gideon pressed a finger to her anus. His warm breath caressed her neck and ear as he used his other hand to grip her shoulder and pull her back as he pumped his fingers into her ass.

Andreas thrust upward at the same time, and it was overwhelming, yet she wanted more.

"Are you ready for me?" he asked her and nipped her neck, sending tiny chills and vibrations down her spine.

"Oh God, Gideon, I'm scared. I want to, but I never before," she admitted.

"You're ready, and you trust me, you trust us to make you happy, to make you ours in every way, and we'll make certain there's only pleasure, not pain."

"Yes. I want it," she said, and then Cerdic cupped her cheeks and brought her closer.

"Take my cock. Suck me, make me yours while we make love together."

His cock was so big, so thick and hard she felt overwhelmed, but then Andreas cupped her breasts and played with her nipples as he thrust his hips.

"Take him now, Sophia. We need you like this. Let go and trust us. Let your desires, your need, lead you," Andreas said.

Her entire body erupted in another orgasm, and she opened her mouth and licked along the base of Cerdic's cock. She knew he wouldn't fit entirely into her mouth. But the sight of his thigh muscles and the scent of his manliness aroused her and led her to take his cock into her mouth. She suckled and relaxed her throat as he gripped her hair, fisted it, and began to slowly ease in and out. She adjusted her throat to his invasion, and then she felt Gideon's fingers pull from her ass, leaving her more needy until she felt something cool and moist press to her ass. He moved slicked fingers in and out and then pulled them out completely. Then she felt the tip of his cock take their place.

"We're yours as you are ours, baby." He eased his cock slowly into her ass. He rocked back and forth.

Andreas lay still, his cock deep in her pussy, and Cerdic began to move in and out of her mouth, making her focus on him, on not gagging and relaxing her muscles. With a plopping sound, she felt Gideon's cock slip into her ass fully to his balls. He exhaled as he rubbed and squeezed her ass.

"Holy God, you're so fucking tight."

"Move, Gideon, I'm already there," Andreas said firmly, and Gideon began to set the pace.

In and out, he slowly fucked her ass. She felt every nerve ending explode around his cock, and then Cerdic grunted and shook as he came in her mouth. She swallowed and licked until he moaned and pulled from her mouth. He gripped her chin and leaned down closer and kissed her. He ran his hand over her ass and then up over her breast. Gideon and Andreas thrust faster and faster, and she cried out her release as Andreas came. Gideon thrust two more times and followed.

"Sophia! Oh God, fucking incredible, Sophia."

She lay against Andreas's chest as Gideon eased out of her ass. Then Andreas caressed her hair and kissed her forehead.

She felt the hands caressing her body, her ass, and she knew it was Lew. His big hands lifted her hips, causing Andreas's cock to slip from her cunt. Andreas gave her a wink and eased off the bed.

On all fours, with Lew pressed over her body from behind, she felt his kisses and his palms exploring her flesh from ass to breasts.

"You're ours now, Sophia. No more secrets. No more hiding. This body, these breasts, this pussy and this ass are ours for the taking, for loving, forever." He reiterated his words with his hands as he stroked her breasts, fingered her cunt, and ran his palms over her ass, letting his finger stroke down the crack.

She pressed her ass back, wanting him inside of her.

"Lew, please. I need you too," she whispered.

Lew cupped her breasts and rocked his hips against her ass.

"You will have me. My way," he said firmly, and she felt her pussy spasm with desire. His hands moved down her shoulders to her hands and wrists. He gripped them as he pressed his much-larger, heavier body against hers.

"I've thought about this moment. Dreamt of touching you, of seeing these big, beautiful breasts overflow my hands." He cupped her breasts from underneath her and kissed her shoulder.

She hung her head, enjoyed his slow movements and the feel of his hands exploring every inch of her body.

He gripped her hips hard, and she gasped.

"I thought of smacking this ass, especially when you lied to us."

"I'm sorry," she whispered.

"Shhh," he said against her neck and over her spine. "Hmm." He pressed his palm over her pussy. "Someone likes the idea of getting spanked."

"I had a feeling she would. I think our girl likes to be naughty," Andreas stated from the side.

Lew stroked a finger up into her cunt.

She moaned.

"Is that right, Sophia? Does the idea of getting spanked by one of us for being naughty get you all turned on and wet?" He thrust a second finger up into her cunt.

"Yes," she admitted.

He pulled his fingers from her pussy and leaned back. "We don't want to scare you, baby. We don't want to be too demanding of this sexy, hot body, but you drive us wild. We want every inch of you, and we want you to give it to us freely, not because we demand it."

"Oh God, Lew, I want you, each of you in every way. I want to feel you everywhere."

He caressed up her thighs to her ass cheeks, squeezed, and pressed them wider.

"Where do you want my cock right now, Sophia?"

"Inside of me."

Cerdic chuckled.

"Oh, she has a lot to learn. But we'll teach her," Cerdic said, and she shivered as her pussy leaked more cream.

Lew gripped her hips and widened her thighs. She felt his cock against her pussy and the crack of her ass.

"Where, Sophia? Where do you want me to take you our first time?"

"Oh God." She moaned and felt her cheeks heat up so hot she thought she must look like a tomato. But her desire, her hunger to get fucked by him next, was overwhelming. He read her body, and he took his time, and she'd never wanted a cock so badly in her life as she had tonight with all four of them.

"Sophia?" he demanded and spanked her ass.

She was shocked and blurted out, "My pussy."

"Oh hell," Andreas said.

Lew kissed her neck and whispered in her ear as he eased his cock into her pussy from behind.

"Good girl, Sophia. Now hold on, you've made me wait too long to make you mine, and I've got to make certain you never forget our very first time."

She cried out her first release as Lew thrust into her pussy in one full stroke. His cock was huge, thick, and hard. Combined with the feel of his iron-clad thighs encasing her thighs as he began a series of deep, hard strokes was enough to make her cream again. She was panting, gripping the comforter as Lew thrust faster and faster. She felt the hand under her chin, and as she looked to the side with half-hooded eyes, she saw Andreas washing his cock with a towel and drying it off, then holding it in his fist, watching her.

She licked her lips and lifted slightly and let the desire lead the way. Andreas winked as he moved closer, bringing his cock to her lips. She took him into her mouth, familiarized herself with his musky scent and began to suck him and move her head up and down.

She felt the other sets of hands on her shoulder and then her breast. She couldn't look but heard Gideon's voice.

"These breasts look awfully lonely, and that's a sin." He then began to lick them and pull and tug and nip with his teeth. She shivered, and Lew grunted as he came in her pussy.

She continued to suck on Andreas's cock when she felt Lew kiss her shoulder and then ease out of her cunt. Cerdic and Gideon had went into the bathroom but now returned. A moment later a tongue licked her anus back and forth and fingers stroked her pussy and trailed the cream to her anus, and then Cerdic gripped her hips and pushed his cock into her ass.

"Oh hell, I fucking can't watch. I can't take it. Her ass is beautiful. She's so giving," Andreas said and then stroked into her mouth and came. She sucked and swallowed, and then he pulled out moaning and groaning.

In a flash Cerdic was lifting her back against him, his cock deep in her ass. Gideon knelt in front of her and pressed her pussy lips apart with fingertips. He held her gaze as she gripped his shoulders and then his head as his mouth descended on her breast. His finger stroked her pussy, and the full sensation was so wild she moaned aloud and came.

"You need a cock in your pussy too, don't ya?" Gideon asked.

"Please, Gideon. Please," she begged.

He lay down, and Cerdic lowered her over him. She took Gideon's cock right up into her cunt, and both men began to fuck her in fast, even strokes. She was losing focus. She'd come so many times already, and now another orgasm was building. She cried out her release.

"Fuck." Gideon grunted, and Cerdic thrust into her ass and held his cock deeply as he came. Gideon followed.

Sophia fell against Gideon's chest. She felt their hands caressing her, their cocks ease out of her, and then the feel of a warm washcloth cleaning her body. Fingers trailed over the tattoo where the M used to be. Then she felt more kisses, more caresses, and then warmth surround her as she drifted off to sleep.

* * * *

"Her body is a work of art. Add in this tattoo and, my God, we're the luckiest fucking men alive," Cerdic said as he ran his fingers along her curves then over the petals of the cherry blossom tattoo. They had showered and were now resting. Sophia fell asleep.

Gideon kissed her forehead and held her hand and wrist against his chest, her breasts flush against his chest as she slept.

Lew stood by the bed, his eyes glued to the spot on her lower back. Gideon knew it bothered him as much at it bothered the rest of them. They were relieved that they could no longer see the branding, just a beautiful, intricate tattoo.

Lew leaned down and kissed her lower back and ran a hand along her full, round ass. "Thank God for Tank's expertise and talent. He helped to give Sophia her life back," he whispered and then stood up.

"I wouldn't go buying him a case of fine whiskey yet. Look how close to her breast that tattoo goes and nearly to the crack of her ass," Andreas pointed out, and Gideon felt his anger rise.

"Fuck, Andreas, really? You needed to bring that up?" Gideon stated.

"It doesn't matter. She belongs to us now. She's our responsibility and our woman to protect and care for. He works alone, so no one else saw her body."

Cerdic chuckled as he leaned down and kissed Sophia's shoulder.

"Funny how possessive and protective we've all become. How do you think she'll be when she awakens?" he whispered.

"Hopefully ready to do it all again," Gideon said, and they all chuckled.

* * * *

Sophia heard their conversation, and she had to force herself not to smile. They were special, each of them, and she couldn't believe she'd made love to four men, that she'd allowed them full access to her body. But she had. She had no regrets. Instead, she felt possessive herself. Those insecure feelings had popped into her head, despite their words of possessiveness and how they couldn't seem to stop touching her body and kissing her skin. She swallowed hard and blinked her eyes open.

"Hey, beautiful," Gideon whispered and gave her a wink. Gideon, with his wavy brown hair, deep chocolate eyes, and that firm, hard muscular jaw, was very attractive.

He lifted her higher, and she felt Cerdic's hands leave her back, and now she was on top of Gideon, her cheek against his chest. She locked gazes with Andreas, who lay on his side wearing only boxers, which just happened to be tented out in the front from his erection. She shyly lowered her eyes and absorbed the feel of Gideon's large hands exploring her back, her hips, and then her ass. Her pussy leaked, and hummed softly as if looking at her body, feeling her skin aroused him.

"I think our Sophia needs us as much as we need her," he said and parted her ass cheeks, running a finger down the crack and over her anus.

She gasped and lifted up, straddling his waist. Gideon quickly gripped her hips, holding her in place. She moved her arm over her breasts to barely cover the nipples.

"Arms down, sweetness. Every part of you belongs to us, and we love looking at this sexy body," Andreas said and reached over to play with her breast.

Her lips parted, and sure enough, she was aroused all over again. Gideon caressed up her thighs back and forth, letting his fingers graze her pussy.

"Have a nice little nap?" Lew asked, kneeling behind her. He pressed his hands over her shoulders and massaged them.

She closed her eyes and moaned. "That feels good, Lew."

Andreas licked her nipple. "I could feast on these all day," he said between licks and bites.

Cerdic cupped her other breast, and Gideon slowly thrust upward. She grabbed onto his waist.

"Are you okay?" Gideon asked her.

"Yes, Gideon."

"No regrets?" Cerdic pushed.

She shook her head.

Lew squeezed her shoulders and whispered against her ear. "We're yours too, Sophia. Get comfortable with our bodies, with knowing that you can take from us what you desire and need. No walls."

She swallowed hard as Gideon lifted his hips upward. Cerdic and Andreas released her breasts, and Sophia eased lower, pressed her ass back, and slowly slid Gideon's boxers down. She held his gaze as her belly slid lower until she was between his legs, lifting his long, thick cock between her hands before she licked it like an ice pop.

"Sweet mother, that mouth is something else." He raised his arms above and under his head, widening his legs as she lifted up and began to suck his cock.

Her body vibrated with such possessiveness and need she felt her pussy spasm. She ran her hands along his inner thighs and felt the iron-hard flesh beneath her fingertips. He was so large, and as she lifted her hips upward, causing her ass to stick out, Lew began to lick her pussy and finger her it.

She moaned against Gideon's cock then felt the hand on either side of her ass. Cerdic massaged the right, and Andreas massaged the left. Then Lew licked her from pussy to anus, back and forth, applying pressure with each swipe and then a stroke of his finger. She rocked a little more, keeping up with the pace as she sucked Gideon's cock deeper. Hands massaged her back and stroked her from neck to ass cheeks, spreading her wider and turning her on more and more.

"Your cream is so addicting, Sophia, and your ass so fucking beautiful. I don't know which one to fuck first," Lew said.

Smack.

She jerked and heard Cerdic chuckle.

"She's teasing you, Lew. Rocking those hips, pressing that ass back in need of cock to fill it up," Cerdic said, and someone stroked a finger into her ass.

"Oh fuck, she sucking my cock good. Whatever you're doing, keep it up. I'm going to shoot my load. Fuck." Gideon continued to carry on and then gripped her hair and lifted his hips.

Smack.

Her body jerked again, and she moaned as Gideon came in her mouth. She swallowed and held on to him until he pulled from her mouth, and then Cerdic wrapped an arm around her waist and pulled her back to the edge of the bed. She thought he would fill her right up with his cock, and she didn't care where he put it. She just knew she wanted it, needed it hard, fast, and now. She was panting, and when no one touched her, she looked around frantically.

Cerdic, Andreas, and Lew were stroking their cocks, standing around the edges of the bed.

Her legs shook, and she began to close them.

"Open for us. Offer us your cunt and ass and that sexy mouth," Lew ordered.

She couldn't move. She didn't know what they wanted her to do. She was on all fours, naked, her ass straight at them.

"Lower down to your belly and lift your ass in offering as you spread your thighs," Cerdic ordered now.

"Oh God," she whispered as her pussy clenched and creamed. She could feel it drip down her inner thighs. But she did as she was told, and one look at Gideon's wide eyes and hungry expression as he lay there in front of her watching gave her the confidence to put on a show and be the woman they'd always wanted.

She slowly lowered to her breasts and belly. Her nipples were oversensitive against the warm bed sheets. She reached between her legs as she spread them as wide as she could without falling and then parted her pussy lips. But before they could touch her, she pressed a finger to her cunt. The sounds they made alerted her to the fact that she'd just turned them on even more. They watched her. She could feel their stares and heard grunting, cursing under their breaths. The temperature in the room rose. She was so in tune with everything.

Then her fingers were pushed away from her pussy, and a tongue replaced them. In and out someone licked her cunt and her ass. She leaked more cream, and then the bed dipped. She felt the thigh between her leg. Lew's hands gripped her ass and hip, and he shoved deeply into her pussy with his hard, long, cock. She muffled her cry of passion into the sheets and placed her hands palms down to brace herself on the bed.

"Oh hell, baby, you know how to set your men on fire," Gideon said, and then Lew pressed her arms forward in front of her as he thrust and rocked into her pussy from behind.

In this position he felt so deep she could hardly catch a breath. She moaned and felt how connected they were with his fingers entwined with hers. She rocked her hips back as best she could and lifted but kept her breasts to the mattress like he'd ordered. Over and over again, he fucked her, harder and harder until he came.

She just caught her breath and felt the smack to her ass as he eased out of her pussy, and then Cerdic was there. He lifted her hips upward so she was on all fours, and then he rammed his cock into her pussy from behind.

"Oh God! Oh, Cerdic!" she cried out and lowered her head as he thrust faster and faster. His arm wrapped around her waist and his hand covered her breast, pinching and massaging her then tugging on the nipple until she cried out another release.

"Fuck she's beautiful when she comes," Gideon said, and she looked up and locked gazes with him. His cock was in his hand stroking it, ready for her again.

"Fuck." Cerdic roared as he shot his load inside of her. He kissed her back and eased his cock out of her pussy.

When Cedric moved to the side, Andreas was there next. He lifted her up, placed her on her back, and pulled her toward the edge of the bed.

"Open for me," he ordered as he knelt down on the floor.

She couldn't move as she lay there catching her breath, legs wide open and hands at her side. Looking down chin to chest, she saw Andreas staring at her pussy and ass. He reached out and stroked a finger up into her cunt. She began to pull her legs together, and Gideon was there to tell her no, placing his hand against one thigh as Lew pressed his palm against the other. Their fingers gently played with her skin, making her shiver and shake with immense arousal.

They were teasing her, getting her wild and needy for more cock.

As Andreas stroked her pussy with fingers, drawing out more cream, Lew and Gideon suckled her breasts, making her spill more cream. When she felt Andreas's finger move to her anus and push right in, she thrust her hips upward and moaned loudly.

"You're so responsive, Sophia. Your body knows our touch already," Andreas said, standing up. He teased her pussy and ass with the tip of his thick, hard cock. He rubbed the muscle back and forth between her pussy lips then to her anus. He applied pressure but didn't push in.

"Andreas, please. I need…" she begged. She actually begged for him to fuck her.

"I can't decide where to go." He tapped his cock against her pussy lips before he dipped it halfway in then pulled right out.

"God damn it, Andreas!" She cried out, and then she felt the cock at her anus slowly push against it and then slide in with a plop. She exhaled, and so did he.

Fingers went to her pussy lips, spreading then and drawing circles over her clit. She rocked her hips as Gideon and Lew held her thighs wide open while Andreas fucked her in the ass with even, slow strokes. His face looked distorted, and her entire body reacted to all of it. To their control, their dominance, and the way four men could love her body and make her beg for cock in every hole.

"Oh!" She moaned and shook as the orgasm overtook her body.

Andreas continued his relentless strokes and then grunted and came.

She absorbed his expression and the way this hard thighs shook from fucking her. Lew and Gideon released her thighs. He lowered down and kissed her lips and then her belly after he eased his cock out of her ass.

She was panting and trying to catch her breath when Gideon slid between her legs and cupped her cheeks. She stared up into his eyes still in some euphoric sexual daze as he slid his cock into her pussy.

She moaned and went to look away as her needy, swollen cunt accepted his cock with ease and desire.

"Look at me. Don't turn away," he said so seriously, and she did.

She stared up into his deep brown eyes seeing flecks of green and such a deep carnal sensation. He eased in and out of her pussy, holding her gaze as he adjusted his body and released her cheeks to raise her thighs higher against his sides.

"I found my new favorite thing to do, Sophia. Do you know what it is?" he asked, thrusting deeper, raising her body to her lower back. Her ass was now off the bed, her shoulders pinned down to the mattress with Gideon over her, encasing her body and fucking her so deeply she could hardly breathe.

"No, Gideon." She barely got that out and didn't look away.

"It's watching you come. You look so amazing. I wish you could see yourself letting go and just feeling. Your ours." He kissed her deeply and then pulled back and stroked faster and faster as he clenched his teeth, and she stared into his eyes.

She felt his cock grow thicker, and she felt her inner muscles begin to spasm.

"Come with me, Sophia. Come now," he ordered, and she moaned as they came together. They both shook and shivered, and he lowered her down, hugged her tightly, and then rolled her to the side. He slid from her pussy, and she moaned softly.

"We'll take care of you, baby," Cerdic said and leaned down and kissed her temple.

"I'll get the bath started," Lew said.

"You're amazing and complete us," Gideon said, and then he kissed her hip while gently squeezing her ass before he began getting dressed.

Gideon caressed her cheek and scattered kisses along her jaw, her lips, and cheeks. The weight of his forearm aroused her nipples, and she realized she was doomed. She'd gone and fallen in love with them and might never get enough of them. They set her heart on fire, and she would never be the same woman again.

Chapter 6

"Are you out of your fucking mind, Jeremy?" his older brother Cody asked him. "Really? The agency is basically saying fuck you because there's a snitch, which means this shit runs deep, and you want to set up surveillance and monitor a commanding official?"

They were sitting in a house in upstate New York. His other brothers, Don and Cooper, had driven up together from the city where they served as trainers in a top-notch fire training facility. They had both done that for several years in the military and were part of an elite arms and explosives division Cody was in the military as well and still worked as a field agent involving terrorist threats.

Jeremy looked at his three brothers. "I've told you everything I've got. You know I went deep under cover. We haven't even spoken for several years because of it. Would I contact you, ask you for assistance if I thought I could trust anyone in the agency right now? Of course not, and the fact that I even have to consider spying on a man I highly respected is killing my gut big time. So, are you going to help me so I can find these two assholes, bring down this criminal organization, and gain back a life for Sophia and myself or what?"

Cooper leaned back in the chair and then took a slug of beer. "I, for one, missed this shit, so you know I'm in."

"Count me in, too. This civilian life stuff gets lame. It's been a while since I've had people wanting to shoot my fucking head off," Don said. Cooper chuckled.

"No one lasted long once they did threaten us. You basically blew them up," Cooper said, and this time, Don chuckled.

"They were bad terrorist assholes who hated us, our country, and everything an American soldier stands for. Fuck them," Don replied.

"Great, now you have these two thinking they're going back into battle against terrorists. This is major shit. We could go to jail," Cody said to Jeremy.

"Only if I'm wrong," Jeremy replied, holding his ground.

Cody exhaled and then ran his fingers through his hair.

"Fuck it. If Jack Banks, your supervisor, a man you and other federal agents are supposed to trust, is aiding these asshole murderers who are after this woman and you, then we'll prove it and bring them down. Tell us what you need, Jeremy."

Jeremy nodded and then looked at his brothers.

"It's going to be tricky, but from what I have thus far, all fingers are pointing to an inside informant. The raid should have been successful. I wasn't there, as I was helping to get Sophia to safety, but somewhere between my call into headquarters and the actual raid, Mateo was tipped off. Deavan very well could have been the main person with the connection to the rat. After all, Mateo hinted about keeping me close to where Sophia was instead of being at the meeting with Scaggs. He also said Deavan met with Scaggs, too."

"Yeah, well, this guy Scaggs is still a free man, despite your boss there, Banks, using all the evidence and proof gathered to arrest him and put him in jail. What happened to all of that?" Cody asked.

"Banks said the higher-ups were after a bigger fish. That's when he hinted about stopping the search for Mateo and Deavan. It was like he was pushing it so that the case would be closed. Meanwhile, my identity is blown, and Sophia is left alone with no resources."

"And you didn't tell Banks or anyone else about Sophia's location?" Cooper asked.

"Only two agents were with me and since then have been transferred from the case. They seemed like good men, but I would think, if they weren't, then Sophia would have been found and taken by now."

"Well, we have our work cut out for us. Should I start with my connections and see if I can get more on this Mateo and Deavan and any close friends or associates who may have helped them to escape?" Cody asked.

"That would be great. Here's a file of some names that popped up on old phone records. I was able to decode the numbers and then had some associates in the agency find out who the numbers belonged to, but before more could be accomplished, the case got the axe." He handed the envelope to Cody.

"Okay. It's a great start."

"And us?" Don asked.

"I need your special skills. That means eyes and ears on Banks, his office, his home, personal cell, his mistresses, everything."

Cooper smiled and rubbed his hands together. "You got it, bro. Let's catch ourselves some scumbag dirty agents."

* * * *

Sophia stood on the deck after they all showered and then made some burgers on the grill and talked about basic things. They discussed the job she had with the local realty company and her hopes to go full time as she learned about the area and what people loved most about Treasure Town.

"Do you have to work the street fair Saturday? Usually all the businesses set up tables with giveaways and promos," Cerdic said as he came to stand next to her by the railing on the deck. She glanced up at him.

"Actually I do but only for a few hours in the morning, then I can look around, too, and learn more about the town."

Cerdic gently ran his palm down her arm as she looked out at the water. It was such a beautiful night, and even though, it was hard to see the ocean at night when it was dark, the sound indicated how close they were to it and how perfect this home was. Cerdic pressed up behind her. He moved her hair from one side of her shoulder to the other then pressed his lips to her exposed skin. She had put the strapless sundress back on because the men said they liked it and hadn't gotten to enjoy her in it.

"You know what I like most about this dress?" he asked as he smoothed his hand along her torso then cupped a breast.

She tilted her head back, giving him better access to her neck and throat as she held on to the railing in front of her.

"How accessible your body is."

She heard the zipper slide down and then felt his large, warm palm slide into the opening and smooth down her hip, straight to her bare pussy. Gideon had warned her about not putting any panties on. It made for a very interesting dinnertime with the men.

"Oh yeah, warm, wet, and ready, just the way I like you." He pressed his thick digit up into her cunt, and she gripped the railing tighter.

"Hold on to that railing. Don't move," he ordered, and then Andreas joined them as her dress began to fall to her waist.

Andreas cupped her breast. "So beautiful. You look like a goddess standing here in the moonlight."

He smoothed his thumb back and forth over the nipple. She didn't moan aloud but, instead, tried to regulate her breathing. She was on fire, and the fact that they would surely have her naked on the porch out in the open aroused something in her. Good thing no other houses were around.

Cerdic thrust his fingers in and out of her cunt.

"I need to taste her, Andreas."

"Inside?"

"No, out here in the moonlight."

He pulled his fingers from her pussy. Her dress fell to the porch deck, and then Andreas lifted her up as Cerdic ducked and then placed her thigh over his shoulder. A moment later, she hung in midair, with Andreas holding her against his shoulder, his hand under her ass and thigh and her other thigh over Cerdic's shoulder while he licked and sucked her cream.

They held her as if her were light as a feather. The fact that she was so high up because of their height, never mind the way her entire body was exposed, made her shake and moan.

"We've got you, baby," Andreas said and moved slightly so he could feast on her breast. That was when Lew and Gideon joined them.

"Relax and let us in," Lew said, and then he tugged on her other nipple with his mouth and placed an arm around her back for support.

She gasped when she felt her right thigh being lifted higher, spreading her wider before she felt the tongue against her anus.

"Fuck I love this ass," Gideon said from underneath her, and then she felt the finger press into her ass. Her body dipped, and she moaned out her first orgasm. Cerdic slurped away.

"Please. Oh God, this is too much. Too wild," she exclaimed, and they chuckled.

"Never too much or too wild. Making love to you will never grow old, baby." Lew tugged on her nipple as Gideon pulled his finger from her ass and Cerdic pulled from her pussy and took her into his arms.

She immediately wrapped her legs around his waist, clasped his face between her hands, and kissed him deeply. She felt aroused and wild with need after what they'd just done to her. They were sexy, strong, and it set her pussy on fire.

He moaned into her mouth and used one hand to hold her under her ass as he undid his pants and shoved them down.

She released his lips, and a moment later, he pressed her against the house and thrust his cock up into her pussy. She moaned as she tilted her head back, giving him access to her breasts, which he suckled and tugged on.

"Fuck, Sophia, you drive me wild. Fuck," he exclaimed as his fingers dug into her flesh and squeezed her ass cheeks apart as he stroked as deeply as he could get.

"Cerdic. Oh!" she exclaimed as she came.

Cerdic pumped four more times and then came, too.

She hugged his neck as he caressed her back then sat down in a long, wide, cushioned recliner.

She didn't stop hugging him, inhaling his cologne, kissing his neck, and he didn't stop stroking her back. They stayed that way for quite some time.

* * * *

Lew sat in a chair and watched Cerdic caress Sophia's back. Andreas pulled a chair close to them, and she reached out and held his hand.

Gideon was in a seat next to Lew, just watching over them as he was, perhaps even thinking what Lew was thinking, how lucky they were to have Sophia as their woman.

As he stared at the tattoo on her body and wondered at how the branches extended and were full and beautiful, the colors as pink and authentic as the actual flower, he felt his chest constrict. Her ex had hurt her so badly. The fact that he was still out there with his buddy and could return to take her from them made Lew's blood boil. He felt so protective and possessive of her. Just looking at her body, voluptuous, sweet, giving, and caring, he knew she had become their center, their world, and everything all in one feminine, sexy package.

He took a deep breath and exhaled, enjoying this moment of peacefulness, of serenity and safety, the scent of the citronella candle burning, the sound of the waves hitting the shoreline, and the feeling that life couldn't get more perfect than right now in this moment surrounded by his family. With that thought came a fear. Deep in the pit of his gut, he felt it sizzle. Something wasn't right. His instincts warned him to be diligent of her safety and protecting of his family, and he vowed to do just that. He would die for her, for them. They were his family, and nothing else mattered.

Chapter 7

"So, it seems some progress was made since we last got together," Frankie teased Sophia as they grabbed some fresh lemonade from one of the stands on the boardwalk. The men weren't too far from them, standing around near one of the entrances to the beach. Cerdic, Andreas, and Gideon had to stand in uniform to represent the marine patrol and do some safety instruction presentations for the community.

Sophia smiled.

"I guess you could say that." She paid for the lemonade then took a sip from hers while the others were being made. She would bring some over to the guys shortly, and then she and Lew would walk around to see some of the other tables set up by local businesses.

"That's so great. I'm happy for you, Sophia. They're great guys."

"They sure are. I really care about them, and I love it here," she said and smiled.

"Well, you fit right in. I've heard great things from Fannie at the real estate agency. Do you like it there?"

"I do, but I would like more hours and maybe get into showing houses, you know, be a little more hands-on. It's hard to promote a place or recommend it if I haven't even been in the place. Plus, I like talking to people and where I lived before I did a lot of real estate work."

"Then it's like a calling for you. You are easy to talk to. I'm certain you would be great. Have you asked Fannie about letting you try that aspect of the job?"

"There are a few other people who got hired before me that do it here and there. I wouldn't want to step on any toes."

"Well, with the way Treasure Town is becoming so popular, I'd say your services would be needed and appreciated, especially since you're ready to work more hours. How do your men feel about it?"

Sophia felt her cheeks warm, and she giggled. "God, I can't believe you just said your men like that. It sounds so weird, yet, feels so right," she admitted.

Frankie gave her a nudge. "Because it is right, and they really care about you. I can see it in their eyes. They light up whenever you're near. Come on. Let's get them the lemonades."

Sophia grabbed the carrier of lemonades as Frankie grabbed hers, and they headed toward their men. They handed them out, and Lew walked over to give them to Cerdic, Andreas, and Gideon.

"You ready for that walk?" Lew asked as he slid his hand around her waist and let his fingers splay slightly over the upper part of her ass in a very sexy, possessive manner. It gave her the chills and made her insides heat up.

"You two have fun," Frankie said and gave Sophia a wink.

Sophia looked toward the set-up where Cerdic, Andreas, and Gideon were. There was a small group of people listening to Andreas present, particularly three young women who were drooling over them. She paused and watched closely, feeling a little jealous. Well, a lot jealous, but then Gideon gave a wave and so did Cerdic and then Andreas. She waved back, and Lew pulled her along.

"Hey, they only have eyes for you."

She looked up into his eyes and then felt that little bit of fear that she wasn't good enough. He stopped her by the bench near the walkway and brought her hands up to his mouth and kissed her knuckles.

"Talk to me. What's wrong? You get this look sometimes like you're so sad or unsure. I don't like it."

"I'm sorry, Lew. I guess I'm feeling insecure," she said and then looked away.

"Hey, look at me."

She looked up into his green eyes. He was six feet four, and even with the heeled sandals she wore today, her head made it only to his chest.

"You're ours, and we're yours. You'll get more and more confident the more time we spend together and get to know one another. Trust doesn't come easy for us either. We're basically opening up our hearts, our bodies to one woman. There's a special bond that we share and always have. It's difficult to explain. But I can tell you that I would die for any of them, and for you. They would do the same. You complete us, Sophia. We're not going to screw that up."

She smiled and then she hugged him when he released her hands.

"Thank you for being honest with me, Lew, and for talking things out. You guys make me happy and make me feel like I can have a life and I'm safe."

"Good, so how about that walk and then we'll meet the guys."

He took her hand, and they traveled along the side streets and saw all the business tables. There was a bit of a crowd gathered near the tattoo parlor. Tank was doing some kind of promotion.

"I wonder what he's giving away," she said to Lew. "Probably a free session or something."

As they got closer, they saw the larger portraits of beautiful tattoos, and he had people signing up for something. Tank caught sight of her at the same time she saw the image that people were talking about, signing a notepad that was under it.

"Sophia," he exclaimed, and she felt her belly tighten. When, not if, Lew recognized the tattoo and the model in the photograph, he was going to flip out. She thought about how jealous and a bit angry they had been that Tank got to see her ass and one side of her breast. How was he going to react to a public display? Thank God her face didn't show.

She gave Tank a hug hello, and then Lew shook his hand. It appeared they knew one another pretty well.

When she felt Lew's hand caress along her hip and then to her ass, pulling her by his side, she had a feeling he realized it was her in the picture.

"What are you doing, giving away tattoos?" Lew asked.

Tank winked. "Hell no, just a free session for a tattoo that requires multiple sessions. When are you coming in to get those angel wings?" he asked Lew.

Sophia looked up at Lew, and he gave her a squeeze closer. "Not sure what I want yet," he replied, and Tank smiled.

"What seems to be drawing all the attention over here?" Lew asked, but he didn't move closer. Instead, he caressed his palm up her waist, gliding up the wire of her bra then back down. He knew it was her tattoo, her body in the picture. Oh God.

"Well, some of my more recent, intricate tattoos are pretty popular. People are signing up to get them."

Sophia was shocked. When they'd come up with the idea together, she and Tank wanted to do something feminine but also something he could work with to hide the branded "M," but she'd never anticipated that women would want it, too.

Tank stepped closer to Lew as he realized Lew was practically scowling as some guys stared at the picture and one guy complimented the body of the model.

"Hey, that was some of my best work ever. Seven days, four-five hours a day, your woman lay there through the pain determined to get her life back. I was honored she chose me."

Sophia felt her eyes well up with tears, and she reached out and took Tank's hand.

"Jeremy was right about your capabilities." She glanced at Lew, who seemed upset but also shocked as he had a firm, serious expression and not a smile. "Because of your abilities and talent, I'm getting my life back, and I have four men I can open my heart up to and trust."

Tank gave her a hug, and then he winked at Lew.

"You and your team better take good care of her. She's a keeper," he said, and then someone called out that they needed assistance with something, and he walked away.

She hugged Lew's arm as they walked by the table, looking at more pictures of tattoos. A few people started showing off theirs, and as Sophia took a step forward, Lew pulled her close to his side, his hand over her hip and moved her along.

"Don't even think about it. You're in enough trouble as is."

She swallowed hard and felt a mix of fear and arousal.

"Lew," she whispered, and he didn't say a word as he pulled her along.

"Later, Sophia, we talk about it."

She stopped short, her heart pounding. He saw her expression and must have realized that he was scaring her. He pulled her close, ran his hand along her ass, and gave it a light tap. He used his other hand to smooth along her neck and chin, tilting her head up toward him. She saw the hunger in his eyes, and that fear in her belly turned into lust.

"You are our woman. We're possessive and protective of what belongs to us and, most importantly, you. You never said you posed for photographs for Tank." He appeared as if he'd bitten the inside of his cheek.

"It wasn't like a photo session. He was proud of his work, so was I, and with all those hours and care going into his work of art, he has a right to be able to show it off so other people can see his capabilities. It's not like you saw my face."

His hand squeezed her ass.

"I could practically see the crack of your ass and the bottom swell of your breast."

She swallowed hard.

"I'm sorry that you're upset. Just for the record, we weren't intimately involved yet."

He raised one of his eyebrows up at her.

"Seriously, you're going to use that as an excuse when you know, at that point, we'd already told you we wanted you?"

"Yes. I wasn't ready because his mark was still on my body and so noticeable. I got that tattoo not only for me, not only to forget and move on, but I got it for the four of you, so that when we make love together, none of you would have to look at another man's marking and—"

He covered her mouth and kissed her. He plunged his tongue in deeply and explored her mouth, stopping her from talking any further. His hand caressed along her lower back, up the side near her breast where the tattoo ended, and then back down over her lower back and ass. It was so intense, and she felt overwhelmed with love for him and for her men.

When he released her lips, he held her gaze. "I love you. He doesn't matter anymore. He can't come between the five of us. You're ours, and this is our body, our tattoo to enjoy, no one else's." He winked.

She felt the tear roll down her cheek. "I love you too," she said and then hugged him tightly.

They then continued to walk, her hugging him around the waist, his hand possessively on her hip as they made their way back to the others so they could all go to dinner and then the Station to hang out with friends.

* * * *

Cerdic snuck up behind Sophia as they got to the house. He was tired from the long day on the beach working the display tables with Andreas and Gideon. As much fun as it was to hang out with their friends, have dinner together and then some drinks at the Station, he couldn't wait to shower and enjoy Sophia. Especially since Lew had told him, Andreas, and Gideon about the photographs at Tank's tattoo shop, how Lew had confronted her on posing and her revealing that she'd done it for them as much as for herself. He was overwhelmed with emotion but also aroused and feeling intense, jealous, and possessive.

"You and I are going into the shower while the others get ready. Then there's a little punishment coming your way for exposing this sexy body and letting Tank take pictures of it," he whispered against her ear as he ran his one hand under her dress and cupped her breast with the other.

"Punishment?" she asked, sounding breathless.

"Fuck yeah," Gideon stated firmly and then clutched her chin between his finger and thumb and lowered his mouth to kiss her.

They weren't even through the front door when Cerdic unzipped her dress and let it fall to the front porch. Gideon cupped both breasts as Cerdic gave her ass cheeks a pinch.

"Ouch," she exclaimed, pulling from Gideon's mouth.

Cerdic pressed her thong panties down and stroked a finger along the crack of her ass. He massaged the round globes as he pressed up against her back.

"You're going to get a nice ass spanking, baby. You're very naughty and need to learn that this body is ours." He stroked a finger up into her cunt from behind, and she moaned softly. He felt her pussy drip cream, and he knew she was aroused. That was how they wanted her, not fearing that they would strike her, hurt her in any way as Lew felt she'd taken his jealousy earlier. He said he'd seen the fear, the uncertainty, in her eyes, and it killed him inside. They would always care for her, put her first, and love her.

"Oh Cerdic." She moaned as Gideon knelt down in the doorway and began to feast on her bare breasts.

"Unless you two are planning to spank her ass and fuck her right here in the doorway, may I suggest we get her in the house first?" Andreas stated.

Gideon stood up and then caressed along her jaw with his finger. Cerdic pulled his finger from her cunt then lifted her up into his arms in a cradle position and carried her inside.

She lay her head against his chest, and when she ran her fingers along his pectoral muscles, his cock grew thick and hard. He got her upstairs, and the others disappeared to shower and get things ready.

"Where did they go?" she asked as he set her feet down on the tile floor in the bathroom and looked at her.

"You trust us, don't you, Sophia?" he asked, and she looked a little scared, but then she nodded.

"Yes."

He gave a soft smile.

"Undress me. I'm yours, just like you're mine."

She looked timid, shy, but then she stepped forward, and damn it, she took her fucking time running her palms up and down his chest. It was torture, and he wished he'd just torn off his clothes, gotten her into the shower, and fucked her so he could gain some self-control. He was obsessed with her, in love with her, and he didn't want to share her with anyone but Gideon, Lew, and Andreas. She belonged to them.

Her dainty fingers lifted the hem of his shirt up and over his head. Then she ran her palms down his chest again, torturing him.

"Sophia, faster," he whispered very intensely.

Her eyes widened, and she undid the belt buckle on his uniform pants, her small knuckles caressing his abs. He couldn't resist cupping her large breasts as he looked at the intricate tattoo on her body. She was so damn sexy and feminine.

"I don't want you to feel jealous. The tattoo was for you as much as for me," she said.

"Lew told us about your conversation. But I am jealous. I don't want any other men seeing what's mine or fantasizing about what belongs to me," he told her firmly.

She undid his pants and pushed them down. He stepped from them and his underwear. She ran her hands along his hips as she looked up into his eyes. She was so petite compared to him. Her head barely came to his shoulders.

"I was jealous today too," she admitted.

He scrunched his eyes together as he caressed her breasts and then her waist. He moved back up and smoothed his thumb along each nipple, making them hard little buds.

"Those women who were drooling over you, Gideon, and Andreas in uniform as you presented the safety seminar. It upset me. One was even licking her lips," she said, sounding so disgusted but looking so damn cute as she scrunched her nose and mouth together looking ready to gag.

He chuckled, and she gave his arm a smack and stepped to turn away.

He grabbed her and lifted her up into his arms, and she straddled his hips.

"Hey, we belong to you. We would never cheat on you or flirt with other women. They mean nothing."

She ran those hands of hers up and down his chest again.

"I hope not," she said, and he shook his head.

"Seems you need a really good spanking tonight," he told her, and she opened her mouth to say something as he reached over to turn on the water in the shower. If they'd been at their house tonight, they could all fuck her in the shower because it was custom-built. But since they'd come to her house tonight, only he could fit in there with her. Their plans at the Station after dinner were turning out well.

He tested the water, and they stepped inside.

He felt so aroused just thinking about spanking her ass and then fucking her with his team. He would never get enough of loving her.

"Why do you guys want to spank me? I thought you said you weren't angry," she said.

He ran his hands along her ass, spreading the globes as he pressed her against the wall.

"Oh baby, we've smacked your ass before during sex, and you liked it. It can be very arousing but also a sign of possession. You got us feeling jealous, and I guess it's our way of securing this bond between us, knowing that every part of you belongs to us. You need to trust us fully and not hold back or lie or keep secrets. You never said that Tank took pictures of you, and you knew we asked about him seeing your body. You had an opportunity to tell us, and instead, you didn't say a word. Your safety, protecting you, this body, is ours. You're still holding back and not giving us all of you. That needs to stop."

"But the four of you are so big. Your hands are huge, and I'm worried that it might hurt. Yet the idea of submitting like that to all four of you arouses me."

He gave her a wink and then reached under and stroked her pussy. Sure enough, she was wet. He leaned forward and kissed her neck, suckling the skin as the water cascaded over their bodies.

"Then you really need this spanking for a lot of reasons. You need to let go and trust us. You need to feel safe, secure, and protected with the four of us always. You need to learn that we would never hurt you, but that every inch of you belongs to us, and if you put yourself at risk, or do something dangerous that could potentially hurt you, then there must be consequences." He thrust his fingers faster up into her cunt. She gripped his fingers.

"Why am I so turned on right now?" she asked.

He slid his fingers out and replaced them with his cock. He held her gaze as he slid into her cunt and thrust the rest of the way in. She gasped.

"Because you know you belong to us, and you want to submit completely to us. That's part of how special this ménage is.

Remember, we love you, and you come first. Submit to us completely, Sophia. Give all of yourself to us, and we promise we'll always love you."

She hugged his neck and kissed him deeply as he stroked in and out of her pussy.

He ran his hands over every inch of her. His desire to possess her, get lost inside of her, was overwhelming. When she started to counter thrust back, he lost his ability to slow down. He pounded into her pussy, squeezed her ass cheeks wider, and she moaned and cried out her release. He followed shortly after and then hugged her tightly as he ran his hands over her ass.

"You're our everything, Sophia. Always."

* * * *

When Sophia walked out of the bathroom with Cerdic, she was sated and well loved. Her legs felt like Jell-O as she anticipated coming into the room to get her ass spanked by her men. It was like going to dungeon, yet her pussy couldn't stop leaking, and her nipples were so hard they ached. She stopped short when she saw Lew sitting on the edge of the bed with his hands on his thighs. Her belly quivered, and she felt the cream drip between her thighs. Cerdic caressed along her hip.

"Go to him," he said to her in a deep voice.

She absorbed the moment before moving. The sight of Gideon, Andreas and Lew in her bedroom naked, looking intense and hungry. The feel of Cerdic giving her hip a tap and her oversensitive body's reaction to even that small touch.

"Sophia." When Lew said her name, she walked to him.

He didn't touch her, just looked into her eyes and then over her body then back to her eyes. Andreas and Gideon moved closer but not next to her. Her entire body hummed with the need for their touch. She wanted it so desperately. She wanted whatever they would give her. *Just touch me already. God. I want their hands on me. I want to be over his lap, I want to feel his large, callused hand spank my ass, and then I want them to fuck me. Oh God, I've turned into a sex-craved maniac.*

"Oh God, I can't believe this. What the four of you do to me. I should be worried, freaking out, but I'm not. I want all of you inside of me. I want to feast on each of you and possess you like you want to possess me. I'm not afraid. I love the four of you, and you're mine. All mine."

She didn't know what came over her, but she fell to her knees, spread Lew's thighs, and immediately licked his cock. She sucked the bulbous head into her mouth, heard him moan, felt his cock harden, and she suckled more, running her hands under his scrotum and cupping his balls, massaging them in her palms.

She heard their reaction.

"Holy fucking shit," Lew said and exhaled then moaned.

"Jesus, I'm going to shoot my fucking load," Gideon said.

"She's amazing," Cerdic said.

"Watch out," Andreas stated, and then she felt her legs being lifted and pillows placed under her knees for height, and a moment later, came the first smack to her ass.

She shivered and shook, moaned against Lew's cock as he gripped a fistful of her hair and rocked his hips. Her dominant action had just turned on her, and now her men were taking full control. She didn't mind at all. If anything, she realized she preferred being submissive and allowing them complete control of her. She just wanted to feel a little control here and there when she could make her men crazy as she sucked their cocks.

She sucked faster, her head bobbing on Lew's cock as she felt the palm caress her ass cheek then a finger slide down her crack and to her pussy. The thick digit dipped in, and she moaned again. It pulled out, and Cerdic gave her ass a few more smacks.

"Holy shit, my turn," Andreas said.

She sensed the movement behind her and then felt the hand smack down on her ass.

"You're ours, Sophia, all ours, and we don't share."

A series of three smacks landed on her ass cheeks, burning her flesh yet making her pussy swell with need. She wanted so much she felt the tears fill her eyes.

"Holy fucking hell. I'm not coming until I'm inside of her," Andreas said, and then she felt his thighs against her thighs, and a moment later, he stroked his cock into her pussy from behind.

She nearly lost her hold on Lew's cock as Andreas slammed into her pussy, thrust after thrust, as he smacked her ass and spread her thighs wider and up. Her feet weren't even on the floor. She felt her belly muscles tense, and she held on to Lew as he thrust into her mouth.

Andreas came with a roar and shook behind her then nipped her shoulder sending goose bumps along her skin. He pulled out, and Lew growled.

"Let go. I want in that pussy when I come," he said gently, tugging on her hair. She released him, and hands lifted her hips.

Gideon placed her on top of Lew, and she sank her pussy down onto his very hard shaft and moaned as she tilted her head back.

Lew thrust upward, making her breasts bounce up and down with his hard, fast upward strokes.

She cried out and then felt her thighs widen and then something cool and thick against her ass.

"You've got my dick so fucking hard, Sophia."

She was incredibly aroused and was coming like a faucet.

"I need you, Gideon."

He cupped her breasts from behind her, moving under her arms.

"You do, baby? Where? Where do you need my hard, thick cock?" he asked and nipped her earlobe, making her moan.

"Tell him," Lew demanded, and she looked at Lew and held his gaze as he gripped her hips.

"Fuck my ass, Gideon. Now," she said slowly and with conviction.

Lew reached up, cupped her neck and cheek, and drew her lower to kiss her deeply. He plunged his tongue into her mouth and ravaged her as Gideon spread her thighs wider. She anticipated the feel of his cock pushing through the tight rings and penetrating her ass. She loved when they all made love together. They were incredibly close and so connected in hearts and souls as one. She shivered and pressed back and heard him chuckle low.

"You want it bad, don't you, baby? You feel exactly what we're felling?" Gideon said and then ran his thumb against her puckered hole and slowly pressed in and out of her anus. It made her so damn wild she thought she might lose her mind. She shook and pressed back.

Lew released her lips but held her against his chest.

"Now, Gideon. Please. Now."

As she got the last syllable out, she felt the tip of his cock at her anus, and then Gideon slowly slid into her ass. The feeling and sensation of completion had her crying out an incredible orgasm. It left her feeling weak, and both Gideon and Lew felt it.

"Holy shit, she's sopping wet. Fuck," Lew grunted and thrust up ward as Gideon thrust into her ass. Lew came first, calling out her name and holding her tightly, and then Gideon thrust four more times and slapped her ass cheeks hard, making her moan and release even more cream as he came.

They lay there breathing rapidly, trying to gain control again, and then she felt her body being moved. Gideon slid out of her ass, and Lew rolled her to her side as he kissed her forehead and her damp cheeks. Then Cerdic was there with a warm washcloth.

"You were incredible, baby. From the shower to the bedroom, you were made for us," he said, and as he washed her up, he kissed along her breasts then down over her tattoo while the others recovered and cleaned up. Cerdic pulled her into his arms and held her.

She was feeling more content and loved than she had ever felt her entire life. Everything was perfect. Her four men had healed her, and nothing could take them away from her. Nothing.

She fell fast asleep in Cerdic's arms.

Chapter 8

"Okay, so what you're saying is that this guy Frederick Price is a friend of Castella Moya, who was very close to Mateo. You have concrete proof that Mateo is in Venezuela and that this Frederick Price is in the States and has had phone conversations with Jack Banks, head of the agency that is supposed to be trying to capture Mateo?" Jeremy asked his brothers Cooper, Don, and Cody.

"That's the gist of it. This is deep shit, too. And, by the way, there are four other agents who seem to have a personal connection to this guy Frederick Price, who also know and have had dealings with Scaggs," Cody told him.

"Holy fucking shit. You guys just busted open a huge investigation. I mean I have to gather all this evidence and pinpoint Mateo's location, Jack Bank's location and Frederick Price's location so we can plan a simultaneous raid. But fuck, who the hell do I trust?"

"Jeremy," Cody said, "I have someone in the government you can trust. Someone you can meet with right away. I just want you to know that I'm sorry I initially tried to talk you out of this. These men involved are badass. They should be dead, never mind behind bars. We'll get everything together, and then I'll talk with my contact and see what reaction I get."

"I appreciate that, Cody. I also have the feeling that this job might just be my last one. I've had it with all this double-spy shit and not knowing who you can trust and who isn't trying to protect this country and the citizens. It's bullshit."

"I hear ya. Let's move our asses on this. If Frederick Price in in the States and associated with Mateo and this Castella guy, then Sophia could be in danger," Cody told him.

"We should head to Treasure Town. We could be of assistance," Cooper added.

"You would find any excuse to visit Treasure Town. You've been wanting to move there for years," Don told him.

"Like you haven't wanted to too?" Cooper replied.

"Let's get all our evidence together tonight, let Cody make the call to his contact, and set up a meeting. Then tomorrow we'll head to Treasure Town," Jeremy said, and they all agreed.

Jeremy prayed that this case was coming to an end and that Mateo and his crew of organized shits was going down. If all went well, he could personally deliver the news to Sophia and her men that Mateo and Deavan were no longer threats to their lives and their futures.

* * * *

Sophia awoke with a fright. The faint smell of smoke had her jerking up in bed. It happened so fast. Her eyes darted to Lew. His eyes wide open, but he wasn't moving. He looked at her all-serious, but it was as if he was paralyzed. Someone grabbed her arm, jerking her upright.

"We're running out of time," the man said to her. She didn't know who he was, but in an instant, she figured it was someone working for Mateo.

She jerked her arm free.

"No. Get away from me," she screamed and jumped on Lew, but he didn't move. She grabbed his shoulders and shook him.

"Lew. Lew!" she screamed, and he just stared at her, eyes wide and moving to the side.

"He'll be no help to you. Will be burned to a crisp after the shit I injected in him. Now come on so you can get dressed," he yelled at her and grabbed for her hair.

She swung her fist, making contact with his face. She was naked, and it didn't even matter. All that mattered was Lew.

The man struck her hard, and she fell against Lew. She cried as she grabbed on to his shoulders, shaking him, trying desperately to wake him up. But then the man grabbed her by her hair and dragged her from him as Lew grunted deeply and growled but was lying still.

She tried fighting the man who held her. He shoved her hard against the wall.

"I can drag you out of here naked. I don't really give a fuck. We leave now, or the other three will die, too. I've got men at their jobs. Their boat is rigged to explode if necessary. Now fucking move it. Sophia," he yelled, and she quickly grabbed her panties off the floor and then stepped into a skirt and tank top that was in the top drawer.

She didn't even get to grab shoes as he took her by her wrist and dragged her from the bedroom. One look over her shoulder and she could see Lew still wasn't moving.

She feared for his life, for Gideon's, Andreas's, and Cerdic's lives. Mateo had found her, and she was as good as dead.

It was dark outside, still early morning, and she remembered the guys complaining about having to leave at four thirty to get to work for five in the morning. They'd wanted to stay in bed with her and made promises of spending the night together and not having to work until Wednesday next week.

The tears streamed down her cheeks as she saw the fire on the side of the house. It was small but would spread fast. What if Lew stayed paralyzed? She tried pulling from the man before they reached the car. "He'll die. He'll burn to death!" she screamed at him. The door to the back seat opened, and she cried out in terror.

"Get in the fucking car, Sophia. We have a long trip ahead of us. The plane leaves in thirty minutes."

Deavan. Oh God no!

* * * *

The call came into the firehouse, and immediately multiple engine companies headed out to the beach house. Jake got the call and the information from Chief Martelli as he was getting up and preparing to head to the department. His heart started to pound immediately, as he feared the men after Sophia had found her.

He got on the phone and tried calling Lew then Andreas.

"Hey, Chief, what's up?" Andreas asked, sounding happy. There was no way he was near the house. How was he going to tell him what was going on?

"Are the others with you? Are you near your house?" he asked as he got into his car.

"What's going on? What's wrong? Gideon and Cerdic are with me. We're at work."

"The beach house is on fire. The call came in a few minutes ago, and I'm on my way. I tried calling Lew and got no answer."

"Oh fuck. We're on our way. We left them in bed at around four thirty or so."

"I'm almost there," Jake said.

"Jake?" Andreas sounded panicked and angry.

"I know, Andreas. I fucking know. Let's hope that they're okay. If not, then you'll need to be here, and we'll get in touch with Jeremy ASAP."

As he hung up the phone and headed toward the road leading to the private area of land and the two beach houses, he saw all the lights and numerous fire trucks. Their friends had gotten there quickly, and the fire was being put out. He saw multiple men carrying out what appeared to be an unconscious man. Was that Lew?

He quickly got out of the car and ran over.

"Is everyone out? Where is Sophia?" he asked Eddie, Lance, and Billy as they placed Lew down onto a stretcher. They covered his naked body, and Jake saw his eyes were wide open and he could barely move.

"He's like paralyzed or something," Hal said to him.

"Sophia wasn't inside. We did a complete sweep of the house," Billy told him.

"Sophia." Lew said her name, all muffled and low.

Jake moved closer.

"Where is she? Did he take her, Lew?" Jake asked.

"Did who take her? What the hell is going on?" Hal asked.

"Hey, we found this on the floor." Eddie Martelli said as he brought over a syringe wrapped in toilet paper.

"Fuck, they drugged him to get to Sophia," Jake said as his deputies arrived.

"What do you need us to do, Sheriff?" Deputy Ronnie Towers and Deputy Turbo Hawkins were there at his side.

"I need you to scan the neighborhood and see who is up and if they saw any vehicles leave this entryway."

"Where is Sophia? What's going on?" Andreas yelled as he, Gideon, and Cerdic arrived.

"They shot Lew up with something. Sophia isn't here. We can't find her," Jake said.

"Fuck!" Cerdic yelled out and ran his fingers through his hair as he began to pace.

"I'm sending my deputies to ask the neighbors if they saw anyone or any vehicles. We'll find her," Jakes said.

"We have video surveillance, cameras everywhere, and installed more when we had to start watching over Sophia," Gideon said and then looked at Lew.

"Find her," Lew said and was beginning to move a little. Cerdic stayed with him as Gideon, Jake, Andreas, and the others ran to their house and the surveillance camera room. Ten minutes later and they had a make of a car and the description of two men. It was a shock when Jeremy and his brothers arrived on scene, armed and ready to intervene.

"Fuck! We're too late. Jesus, did you stop them?" Jeremy asked the gathered men.

"They got her. What the fuck is going on?" Andreas said, and then Gideon handed the papers with the photos over to Jeremy.

"That's one of Frederick Price's men," Jeremy said to them. Gideon handed him the other one, which was a little blurry.

"Oh Fuck. Fuck, fuck, fuck!" Jeremy exclaimed and ran his hands through his hair.

"Who the hell is it?" Jake asked.

"That's fucking Deavan. He's the one that believes she belongs to him and Mateo. He's the one from that night," he said to Andreas, Gideon, and Cerdic.

"I'm going to kill these motherfuckers," Cerdic stated aloud.

They heard a roar and then men curse as a stretcher tipped over. Jake and the guys hurried to Lew, who was growling and trying to fight through the shit they'd injected him with. His face was red, his fists at his side as he forced himself up slowly from his knees to a standing position.

"Jesus, Lew, I don't think you can force it out of your system that fast," Paramedic Johnny Landers told him.

"Fuck that. I'm gonna kill that piece of shit. He struck her, dragged her from me. She was so scared, and I couldn't do shit but lie there like a fucking zombie. They knew. They fucking knew I could take them, and they fucking stuck me in the neck. I didn't hear them enter until it was too late, and now they have Sophia. We need to get to her. Now."

"Hey, Jeremy," Cody said, "we've got some info. Seems that person I hooked you up with is also helping to run a larger investigation, and Price, Ruiz, and Castella are on the wanted list. As soon as Price and Deavan Hoyt entered the U.S. from Venezuela, an alert was issued. But since we've been putting together this case to lock these shits up, they weren't tailed until thirty minutes ago when they boarded a private jet."

"She's on that plane?" Andreas asked.

"Getting confirmation on that but let's assume yes because Deavan and Price are," he replied.

"They're headed back to Venezuela?" Chief Martelli asked as all the men and their friends gathered around them.

"They're headed to Peru. That's what they got from air traffic control."

"What's the plan of action?" Jake asked.

Jeremy looked at Sophia's men. "Cody?" Jeremy asked his brother.

"Grab your Navy SEAL gear," Cody said. "It's going to take days for the feds to get organized. I'll work on the logistics and protocol issues with our contact. In the end, all they'll give a shit about is getting these people out of the United States. Sophia won't be alive in forty-eight hours, and finding her in a place like Peru is not going to be easy."

"If we all work together, it will be," Nate said, joining them and dressed for action in black fatigues, a black T-shirt, and a Glock. "The plane leaves in thirty. Grab your shit."

"Nate, what's your plan?" Jake asked him. Nate looked between the men.

"We're taking care of this on our own. No feds fucking it up, no bullshit. Sophia deserves happiness and to be free from this asshole. You guys clean up the mess around here. We're going to get Sophia back to where she belongs. With her men in Treasure Town. Let's move."

* * * *

Sophia was moaning in pain. She wasn't sure how long she had been here, or even where here was. Her body ached, her lips and cheeks swollen, her legs battered and bruised after Deavan and Mateo beat her. She wanted to die, to just pass out and never wake again.

They'd told her Lew had died in the fire and that they'd blown up the marine patrol boat that Gideon, Cerdic, and Andreas were working on. She cried for them, and that just added to her punishment.

She wondered why they hadn't raped her. They'd touched her, told her they would do things, but still, they hadn't yet. It was as if they were trying to cleanse her body and got more pleasure out of torturing her and striking her, hearing her suffer. They were sick, sadistic bastards, and if she got the chance, she would kill them and without a care of dying in the process. There was nothing to live for.

Her head so fuzzy she couldn't even think a full coherent thought. Maybe she had a concussion. She'd passed out too many times to remember, and even now, she lay here tied to the bed but unable to move a muscle. She moaned and wanted to cry, but there were no more tears to shed. As she glanced toward the right, she saw the evening approaching. Would they come back to her as they promised and hurt her more? She heard the door open, and her heart didn't even pound so hard anymore. She had given up.

Mateo approached, carrying something. Deavan came in, too, wearing no shirt and holding some sort of flat, long stick in his hand. He stared at her and slapped the stick against his hand, making a snapping noise.

"We need to take care of a few things, Sophia, before we make you ours again," Mateo said to her. He was busy setting something up on the table. When she saw the flash of fire from a lighter then something enflame, she shook with fear and thought about Lew. Her heart ached. She wished she had died with him.

"As much as I enjoy the new ink on your body, it seems to be missing something special. Something that indicates who exactly you belong to."

The slap from the stick landed across her thighs, and she cried out.

"Pay attention. They'll be no running this time," Deavan said and then made her jerk, anticipating another strike from the stick he held, but instead, he ran the flat tip of it between her legs over her belly to her lips.

She heard the hiss and turned away to see what Mateo was up to. When she saw the branding tool she cried out and shook her head. "No. Not again. No. You already did that to me."

"Untie her," he ordered. "I want it on her back where it belongs and where it was before."

Deavan pulled out a knife. He dropped the stick on the bed and undid her legs first and then her hands. He gripped her tightly as he flipped her onto her back. She was crying and begging for them not to do it.

Mateo gripped her cheek. "But they're dead, all four of them, and you're ours again. Submit to me, to us, and your treatment will improve. Your punishments will be over."

She thought about it. If she played up to their control, they might let their guard down. She was alone in this, and she wanted to die. She had nothing to lose.

"They're dead. They're not coming. This is your life now. You're with us forever," Deavan said and ran his hands along her ass and her back. He pressed a finger between the crack of her ass, and she shivered.

"Okay. Okay, I'll submit. I accept you both," she said. Deavan eased up, and Mateo smiled.

"Smart choice," he said, and he pulled her to standing position. He kissed her shoulder.

"Bend over the bed and offer me your body to brand."

The lights went out, and Sophia didn't know what was happening, but she made a move. She kicked back with all her might and heard Mateo grunt. She reached for the branding tool and turned and swung at him, hitting him in the face. The strike to her arm with the knife made her scream, but she just kept swinging the hot branding iron and heard Deavan roar as it made contact with his skin. The stench of burnt flesh filled the air, and the strike to her face had her falling back against the wall. The branding iron hammered to the floor and skittered across it, and then hands gripped her throat, and she struggled to get free. Deavan lifted her by the throat and tossed her onto the bed. She cried out, screaming and fighting him as shots of light illuminated the room. Deavan fell from her body, and then Mateo roared. She could barely stay conscious, but then she felt the strong arms pulling her off the bed. A man in black wearing a black mask. He had deep green eyes.

"We've got you, baby. We're going home. Stay with us now. Your men are here."

"Lew?" she whispered, and he told her to be quiet, and she was.

He was alive, the others, too. She sensed them near her as they descended the stairs and stepped over things. She didn't know what until the light from the moon illuminated the stairway landing, and she saw the bodies and the blood. They'd killed them. Her men had come in and rescued her. They weren't dead. She fought to stay conscious and to be quiet as Lew carried her, followed by a team of other men in black. But there were six of them. Who else was with her men?

She closed her eyes and held on as best she could. The movement and the feel of tree branches hitting her battered body made her moan.

"Shhh, baby. Please be nice and quiet," Lew said to her, and she gulped the pain down and held on with the little strength she had left.

It was so dark. How could they see? She heard a door open then the low hum of an engine. They were in a vehicle, and no one said a word. Lew just kept her pressed against his chest. She phased in and out of consciousness. Then she heard water and felt as if she was on some kind of raft or something.

"How is she holding up?" Andreas asked. But he didn't touch her. No one but Lew had touched her, held her, and she wondered why. But suddenly she felt so weak, and she just couldn't keep her eyes open. It was as if the adrenaline left her body, and that was it.

Chapter 9

"This is Catalina, a friend of Frankie's and the girls. She's a nurse that works in the ER. Let her take a look at that flesh wound," Jake told Jeremy as he sat in the chair in the waiting room waiting to hear how Sophia was doing. His brothers were there, too, and the moment he caught sight of Catalina, he didn't argue with Jake.

"It's not a big deal. We wrapped it up, and it's nothing. I've had worse," Jeremy said.

"Why don't you let me be the judge of that? Sophia hasn't awoken yet, so you have some time," Catalina told him firmly, and he was aroused and completely attracted to the woman. When he felt Cooper next to him, giving him a nudge as he winked at Catalina, he was shocked.

"Come on, bro, let's let the sweet, beautiful nurse make sure you won't need that arm amputated," he teased, and Catalina chuckled as Jeremy and Cooper headed to a room with Catalina as Don and Cody continued to handle the negative results of their gung-ho, John-Wayne tactics that had saved their friends' woman before the feds could get her killed.

He pretty much knew his career in the government was over, and he didn't give a shit. When he heard what Mateo and Deavan were planning on doing to Sophia and then heard her cries and her fighting for her life, he knew he'd made the right decision in accompanying his friends and heading to Peru after her. Cerdic, Andreas, Lew, and Gideon were very resourceful Navy SEALs. He and Nate were truly impressed and grateful, as they'd kept them alive under circumstances he and Nate weren't exactly familiar with. It gave him a new-found respect for Navy SEALs and specifically for the four men who shared Sophia and loved her so much they risked their lives, their careers, and their future for her. It made Jeremy think about himself and his brothers, their lives, their careers and what they hoped for in the future. Maybe it was time to start looking into settling down?

As Catalina bent over to grab a pen that Cooper dropped, Jeremy absorbed the shape of her round ass, the cute nurse's uniform, and then the way Cooper had his arms crossed, smiling. Maybe he and his brothers could find happiness in Treasure Town too?

* * * *

It actually felt really relaxing to sit in the hot tub and just soak and rest. The last several weeks had been hectic and tiresome. She was constantly in pain and recovering from her internal, as well as external, injuries. Thank God nothing was too serious, although her men considered every mark, every bruise unacceptable, and they looked her body over day and night, watching to make sure she was healing well. But right now, as she lay in the tub, her face pointed up toward the evening sky, she felt so relaxed she could have fallen asleep. This hot tub was way bigger than the one at her beach house across the way, which was now under construction. Nate and Rye were doing all the new construction, and she got to stay with her men in their house as she recovered and they dealt with the results of their unauthorized mission to save her life.

But she had helped them get out of trouble when she offered information to the feds she hadn't realized was important until she started remembering passwords and codes she'd overheard. Jeremy didn't even know, and ultimately, it saved them all from getting put in prison.

"You shouldn't stay in too long. I don't want you feeling any pain," Lew told her as he appeared by the Jacuzzi, wearing only shorts and a T-shirt. The others came outside, too, and were all holding beers.

They looked so serious still, and she wanted them to know she was okay.

"It feels good, Lew. I don't feel any of the aches and pains while I'm in here."

"Really?" he asked.

She smiled. "Yes. So why don't you guys come join me? I love having you close to me, you know that."

Immediately they were pulling off their shirts and coming into the Jacuzzi with their beers. She had a nice tall glass of lemonade on the shelf behind her.

Lew leaned over and kissed her lips and then her shoulder. Cerdic moved in on her other side and kissed her other shoulder and then Andreas and Gideon sat across from them and both teased her feet with theirs. They were all touching, all together, just like she loved.

"So you think the hot tub is healing you?" Andreas asked.

She looked at him and then all of them.

She shook her head.

"No?" Gideon asked, filled with concern.

It was so hard not to look at each of them and get aroused and turned on. Especially as she remembered what they'd risked to get to her and save her and how sexy and sinful they'd looked dressed in black SEAL gear as they killed the bad guys, destroyed all chances of Mateo and Deavan ever hurting her again, and got her to safety. They were her true heroes, her everything.

"I love you guys so much. I appreciate all you do for me and trying to make me feel better, but the truth is, this tub, the resting, the painkillers aren't what's healing me. It's the four of you. You're all I've ever wanted, the reasons why I'm alive right now, and my motivation to get better and to have a happy, loving future with you. You heal me. You complete me, and I'll love you with all my heart, body, and soul, forever."

"We love you, too. In fact, I could use some loving of that body right now," Andreas said, and he pulled her forward with his legs.

She nearly went under the water, but he pulled her into his arms and hugged her tightly. When lips kissed her shoulders and back and then fingers maneuvered under her bathing suit and straight into her pussy, she moaned and began to rock her hips. She was the luckiest woman in the world with four men who had set her heart on fire and healed her soul forever.

THE END

WWW.DIXIELYNNDWYER.COM

ABOUT THE AUTHOR

People seem to be more interested in my name than where I get my ideas for my stories from. So I might as well share the story behind my name with all my readers.

My momma was born and raised in New Orleans. At the age of twenty, she met and fell in love with an Irishman named Patrick Riley Dwyer. Needless to say, the family was a bit taken aback by this as they hoped she would marry a family friend. It was a modern day arranged marriage kind of thing and my momma downright refused.

Being that my momma's families were descendents of the original English speaking Southerners, they wanted the family blood line to stay pure. They were wealthy and my father's family was poor.

Despite attempts by my grandpapa to make Patrick leave and destroy the love between them, my parents married. They recently celebrated their sixtieth wedding anniversary.

I am one of six children born to Patrick and Lynn Dwyer. I am a combination of both Irish and a true Southern belle. With a name like Dixie Lynn Dwyer it's no wonder why people are curious about my name.

Just as my parents had a love story of their own, I grew up intrigued by the lifestyles of others. My imagination as well as my need to stray from the straight and narrow made me into the woman I am today.

For all titles by Dixie Lynn Dwyer, please visit
www.bookstrand.com/dixie-lynn-dwyer

Siren Publishing, Inc.
www.SirenPublishing.com

Lightning Source UK Ltd.
Milton Keynes UK
UKOW06f1931010817
306490UK00014B/798/P